Margaret Wade Campbell Deland

Mr. Tommy Dove, And Other Stories

Margaret Wade Campbell Deland

Mr. Tommy Dove, And Other Stories

ISBN/EAN: 9783743302990

Manufactured in Europe, USA, Canada, Australia, Japa

Cover: Foto ©Andreas Hilbeck / pixelio.de

Manufactured and distributed by brebook publishing software
(www.brebook.com)

Margaret Wade Campbell Deland

Mr. Tommy Dove, And Other Stories

MR. TOMMY DOVE

AND OTHER STORIES

BY

MARGARET DELAND

AUTHOR OF "JOHN WARD, PREACHER," "SIDNEY"
"THE STORY OF A CHILD," ETC.

BOSTON AND NEW YORK

HOUGHTON, MIFFLIN AND COMPANY
The Riverside Press, Cambridge
1894

The Riverside Press, Cambridge, Mass., U. S. A.
Electrotyped and Printed by H. O. Houghton & Co.

CONTENTS.

MR. TOMMY DOVE.

I.

THE apothecary shop in Old Chester stood a little back from the street. There was a garden in front of it, but the fence which inclosed it was broken in places, so that an envious hand, had any such been known in Old Chester, could easily have broken off a cluster of cinnamon roses, or grasped a stately stem of tall white lilies.

The shop itself was but the square front room of Mr. Tommy Dove's old stone house. One of the windows had been cut down to make a door, so that customers might not wear out the white-and-gray oil-cloth in his mother's entry; and the two front doors, side by side, were perhaps more of a distinguishing feature than the small pestle and mortar, which, suspended by wires from an upper window, had long ago given to the wind and rain whatever gilding they possessed.

It was since Mrs. Dove's death that the fence

had fallen out of repair, and wayfarers might
be tempted by the bloom and richness of the
garden; and since her death, too, the real front
door had not been opened, and gradually the
gray house had lost its individuality as a home
to become merely the apothecary shop.

Yet, in spite of the closed shutters of the upper rooms and the silent entries, Tommy Dove
still tried to feel that he had a home. He was
glad to close the shop at night, first arranging
the cord of the jangling bell, that he might be
summoned if he were needed, and then going
into the kitchen, to eat, all alone, the somewhat
uncomfortable supper which had been prepared
for him by the woman who took charge of the
house. He would open a book beside his plate,
and eat, and read, and dream, until Mrs. Mc-
Donald's heavy step warned him that she was
impatient to put the kitchen to rights for the
night. After she had gone, and everything was
in stiff and uncomfortable order, Tommy would
rub his hands together, and listen to the kettle
singing on the fire, and think how cozy he was,
and how independent. But these moments of
satisfaction held always a strange consciousness
of disappointment in himself, for he was not
mourning for his mother! Anybody who knew
anything about the late Mrs. Dove would have
said "No wonder!" — but her son, who knew

more than any one else, felt only his own loss in
being unable to grieve for her. He did not
understand the pang of regret for an unfelt sorrow, the human claim for the human experience;
he only knew vaguely that he was missing some
richness in his life, and there was always the
effort to drive his thoughts back to his own loneliness.

"Ah, it's hard on a man to have to make his
own tea and look after his household affairs,"
he would remind himself, ashamed and remorse-
ful because of his content.

It pleased the apothecary to say "household
affairs," and it pleased him yet more to meditate
upon them in silence, with no shrill interrup-
tions or commands. After long repression and
distrust, it was with a kind of wondering joy
that this obedient son found the keys of the
china-closet and the linen-press in his posses-
sion. True, their contents had no especial
value, — "An ill-favoured thing, sir, but mine
own." He counted the sheets and pillow-cases,
and laid fresh sprigs of lavender among them
with his own hands, and he cautioned Mrs.
McDonald to be careful in washing the old blue
cups and saucers. He wished that she would
not always reply, "Yes, yes, Mr. Tommy.
Don't fret, dear." She meant it kindly, he
was sure, but it hurt his new-born dignity a
little.

"If mother had only called me 'Thomas' instead of 'Tommy,'" he thought, "people would have treated me with more respect."

But, if a man's own family snub him, he need not hope for anything more reverent than kindness from his immediate world. In a vague way Mr. Tommy realized this, and accepted the friendly nickname without a protest.

Part of the joy of being free, of being able to do as he liked, expressed itself in the apothecary's garden. While his mother was alive he had been obliged to rise early and work hard, and prune and train his plants according to Mrs. Dove's ideas. But now he no longer started at the whir of his alarm clock at four in the morning, dearly as he loved his garden, and much as he missed those hours of the misty dawn among his flowers: the tropæolums should trail halfway across the gravel path, if they wanted to; and the sweet peas might clamber up into the white rosebush, if it pleased them; Tommy would not train them. He sometimes thought he knew how they had felt in those days of precise order. The broken fence did trouble him a little, but that it should not be mended was his unconscious protest at the past.

Yet he did bestir himself in this matter a week before the Temples came back to Old Chester. He was unwilling that Mr. Temple

should notice any disorder about the shop, or
that little Dick Temple should find the garden
such a tangled growth that he could not see the
seeds of the balloon-vine which he used to love
to crack against his rosy cheek; nor could he
bear to have Miss Jane think that he neglected
his plants. So it was really a relief to him,
when he sat down at his tea-table one June
evening, to know that the fence was mended,
and not a single weed was hidden among the
flowers. He seated himself by the open kitchen
window, and, rocking slowly back and forth,
stirred his tea with a small, thin spoon. The
morning-glory leaves outside made a frame for
the distant hills, and for the yellow sunset with
its filmy bars of gray cloud. Tommy was thinking how long it was since the great house at the
other end of the village had been opened. Yes,
it was surely eight years since the Temples had
been in Old Chester.

He tried to adjust his thought of Dick.
"Why, he must be quite a boy," he said. "And
there was a baby girl, too. I suppose she has
grown a great deal." He felt a kindly, simple interest in all the family; and then he reflected that the Temples would sympathize with
him because of his mother's death. That they
knew all about it the apothecary did not doubt.
Was it not the most important event of his life?

He wondered if Miss Jane had changed much; he even sighed a little as he thought of her. Miss Jane Temple, living in her brother's rich, comfortable house, with strong, bright interests all around her, seemed to this silent and somewhat timid man like a being from another world. Henry Temple's light-hearted indifference to everything outside of his own life had always awed the apothecary; but Miss Jane, in spite of her different world, was not like her brother, — she was kind, Tommy Dove thought, and gentle; so that when he saw her alone, on those rare days when she came to the shop, he was not at all afraid of her.

"Yes," he said to himself, putting his cup and saucer down on the window-sill, "I should n't wonder a bit if she came in to tell me she sympathized with me, she's so kind."

And he was right in thinking Jane Temple would condole with him. She heard of Mrs. Dove's death soon after her return, and, knowing less of the character of the deceased than most of Old Chester, she came very soon to the apothecary shop to say, with tears in her eyes, that she had heard of Mr. Tommy's loss, and she was so sorry. She was thinking of her own mother as she spoke. "It is very sad for you, Mr. Tommy," she said; "I — I know how sad it is."

She had walked up the smooth gravel path with little Effie Temple hanging upon her hand, and she stood now at the low stone step. Mr. Tommy, leaning on his half-door and looking absently at the bloom and tangle of his garden, had straightened up as he saw her coming, and hurried out to take the hand she extended, and to stumble through some sort of greeting.

"And who is this little girl?" he inquired, buttoning his coat up to his chin with nervous fingers. The child's calm stare disconcerted him even more than Miss Jane's presence.

"This is my niece Effie," Miss Jane answered, smiling, for the little girl did not speak. "She was a baby when we left Old Chester."

"Oh, yes," replied Mr. Tommy, — "oh, dear me, yes, indeed. I remember there was a baby. Won't you step in, Miss Jane? — and perhaps the little girl will let me make some hollyhock ladies to amuse her?"

Effie frowned, but looked interested. "What are hollyhock ladies?" she demanded.

Her aunt did not go into the shop, though Mr. Tommy held the half-door hospitably open.

"I will just wait here," she said; and so while Mr. Tommy went over to the row of hollyhocks, and stood bareheaded in the sunshine, filling his hat with the silky blossoms, white and buff, rose-color and deep wine-red, she sat

resting on the warm, broad step. She watched
the row of pigeons sunning their white breasts
on the ridgepole of the barn, and listened to
their long, rippling coo. A shadow from the
honeysuckle about the door blew back and forth
across the path, and up from the garden came
the scent of sweet alyssum and mignonette.

When Mr. Tommy came back, Effie, with
her hands behind her, and grave, unresponsive
face, watched him strip off the calyx and bend
back the petals, leaving a puffy yellow ball with
nodding plumes upon a slender neck. The
apothecary's fingers seemed all thumbs under
the calmly critical gaze of the child, but he
managed to tie a blade of grass around the
middle of the folded petals.

"That is a sash," he explained nervously.

"I don't think," Effie observed slowly, "that
anybody would know they were intended for
ladies."

"Oh, Effie, dear!" said Miss Jane plead-
ingly.

But Tommy hastened to agree with the child.
"Oh, no," he said. "Oh, dear me, of course
not. They don't look at all like ladies. But
when I was a little boy I used to think they
did, and I made whole families of them when
the hollyhocks were in blossom; they were my
dolls, you know."

"I did n't know boys played with dolls," Effie answered.

Miss Jane looked distressed and apologetic; and it was perhaps because she feared Mr. Tommy's feelings had been hurt that she went through the shop into the small sitting-room beyond, and listened while he told her of his mother's sickness and death. But Effie's presence embarrassed him so much that, with a nervous desire to propitiate her, he opened the door of a corner-closet and took out a cup and saucer of thin, fine china. There were little faded lavender flowers scattered over it, and the gilt upon the handle was somewhat worn, but it was delicate and pretty, and Tommy, standing in a streak of sunshine, with one lean hand upon the door of the closet, looked with wistful blue eyes at Effie.

"Perhaps," he said, "the little girl will take this little gift. I should be pleased if she would accept it."

"Oh, it is so pretty, Mr. Tommy," said Miss Jane. It would not be kind to decline it, she thought, since Effie had been so naughty. "Say 'thank you,' Effie," she instructed her niece, who was holding the cup in silence; "Indeed, you are too good, Mr. Tommy; it 's *very* pretty!" she ended, with nervous emphasis. And, in her mild way, as they walked home, she reproved the child because she had not seemed pleased.

But Effie was never known to hesitate for an excuse.

"Well, but, aunty," she explained, "why should that man give me a cup and saucer? Haven't we *hundreds* of cups and saucers? And he kept calling me 'little girl,'—and his ridiculous old hollyhock ladies!"

II.

This little visit of Miss Jane's gave Tommy Dove much to reflect upon.

How gentle she was, how low her voice, how condescending her manner! Mr. Tommy knew no better than to call Miss Jane's timidity condescension, but that did not make him less happy. There was no one in Old Chester in the least like her, he thought; and then he fell to meditating upon his loneliness. He wondered how life would have seemed if his mother had not hated Mary Ellen Boyce, and the one dawn of love in all his cramped years had been allowed to brighten into day. Yet, curiously enough, he found himself regretting his mother's sternness less than he had ever done before.

He thought of his talk with Miss Jane so often that week that, without quite knowing why, he found himself, at the close of the Wednesday evening lecture, waiting outside the church door.

Miss Jane, stopping to speak to old friends, was so long in coming out that when she reached the steps most of the congregation had dispersed; so Tommy, quite naturally, began to walk beside her as he said, "Good-evening," and hoped that she "found herself very well."

Miss Jane answered with a gentle cordiality which the apothecary thought beautiful, but she stopped, and glanced back at the church, and then looked anxiously up the moonlit road, which wound like a white ribbon back among the hills. "I asked Dick to meet me," she explained, "but very likely he has forgotten it. He is such a good boy, Dick is, but sometimes he forgets." Miss Jane's love was not of the fibre which demands the best in its beloved.

"If," said Mr. Tommy eagerly, — "if you will allow me to walk along with you, ma'am " —

"Oh, no, indeed, Mr. Tommy," she answered, quite fluttered and hesitating. "The lane is as quiet as can be, and the moon has made it as light as day."

But the apothecary urged her again with respectful anxiety. "You ought not to be alone, if you 'll allow me to say so, Miss Jane." And so he went to the very door of Henry Temple's house. Miss Jane had so many questions to ask about Old Chester, and he had so much to tell her, that the walk was a pleasant one to them both; and, with a friendly impulse, as she said good-night and thanked him for his kindness, she asked him if he would not come in.

It was with a strange sensation that, standing in the shadows at the foot of the white steps, Tommy Dove declined what he had never dreamed would be offered to him. But he did decline it, and then went back to his shop, and, sitting down behind the counter, leaned his head on his hands and thought it all over. He hoped that he had expressed himself well in talking to Miss Jane; — "elegantly" was the word in Tommy's mind. He felt sure that his conversation about his books had been genteel, but he doubted a little if it had not been vulgar to speak of such things as the snails and rose-bugs in his garden. This troubled him, and he was not quite happy when he lighted his candle and went upstairs to his bedroom under the eaves.

Miss Jane had enjoyed the walk home, but she was a little relieved that Mr. Tommy had not accepted her invitation. "There are no lights in the parlor," she said to herself, "and I could n't have taken him into the library."

When she opened the library door, her sweet face, no longer young, glowing a little from the cool air, and her eyes dazzled by the light, Henry Temple glanced up at her over his glasses long enough to say, "Well, Jancy?" and then

settled back into his newspaper; but Dick
sprang up from his seat beside his mother's
sofa with a conscience-stricken look.

"Oh, aunty," he exclaimed, "what a lout I
am! I forgot all about your prayer-meeting!'"

"Why, Richard!" said his mother in dismay,
and Mr. Temple put down his paper to say,
"Were you to go for your aunt? I'm ashamed
of you, sir!"

"Oh, it is no matter, dear brother," protested
Miss Jane, her face shining with affection.
"Never mind, Dick. As though one could n't
come home alone in Old Chester! — though,
really, I did n't come home alone. Mr. Dove
walked back with me."

"Dove?" said Henry Temple. "Oh, Mr.
Tommy? Yes. Well, that was very nice in
the little man. Did n't his mother die last
winter? Dick, you cub, have you apologized to
your aunt? Jancy, while I think of it, just see
that my gun-case is mended, will you? The
baize is torn at one end."

"And, aunty," Dick said penitently, "if
you 'll forgive me this time, I 'll go with you,
as well as for you, next week. It 's this beastly
translation; just look at that stuff! — '*Findi-
tur nodus cordis*'" —

Miss Jane took off her bonnet, and leaned
over Dick's shoulder. Ever since the days in

which she taught him his A B C's, she had been impressed by her nephew's learning; but she did not comment upon it now.

"Yes, she died in January," she said slowly. "He must be very lonely."

No one answered her; each member of the family had his or her occupations and interests, and Miss Jane's pity was as unnoticed as the fall of a rose-leaf outside in the tranquil night.

The library was such a pleasant room, though it was dim with cigar smoke that evening, that it was easy to shut out other people's affairs and be simply comfortable. The window on the south side had a broad, leather-cushioned seat, where Effie Temple was curled up reading by the light of a hanging lamp. The windows were open, and the soft June air and the climbing roses came in together from the moonlit night. The walls were lined with books, and in the corners were racks for fishing-rods; a pair of spurs had been thrown down upon a table littered with papers and letters and bits of unfinished fancy-work. A liver-colored pointer had fallen asleep beside Mrs. Temple's sofa, her delicate hand resting lovingly on his sleek head, and a collie was stretched at the feet of the master of the house.

Miss Jane felt, vaguely, that this careless comfort was the reason of the indifference to the outside world. Mr. Tommy's sorrow could not touch any one here, and for that reason, perhaps, she kept it in her own heart; and, possibly because the interests of her life were not her own but other people's, Miss Jane's heart had room for Mr. Tommy's griefs.

"Really," said Mrs. Temple that night to her husband, after she had eaten the bowl of delicate gruel her sister-in-law had brought her, — "really, Janey is a great help; you have no idea how much, in a small way, she relieves me."

"I've not a doubt of it," responded Henry Temple, pausing with his bootjack in one plump white hand. "Janey has n't any mind, particularly, but she is a very good sort of person to depend upon. It's lucky she never married."

"Well," said Mrs. Temple doubtfully, "it is fortunate for us, Henry — but perhaps — don't you think that for Janey it is not so pleasant? I am almost sorry for Janey. Not but what she is contented, — in your household, she could not be anything else, — but a woman is happier to be married, my dear."

She smiled at him adoringly. Possibly her sister-in-law's usefulness had contributed to Euphemia Temple's view of the happiness of matrimony; it had certainly protected her ideal of her husband, and kept her blind to certain facts of temper and selfishness, which, if the

housekeeping machinery had not run smoothly,
or his comfort had been interfered with, she
must have learned. "No unmarried woman
knows what happiness is!" she declared. Her
husband laughed, — Mr. Temple's laugh was so
frequent and so cordial that people said he was
the most good-natured fellow in the world.

"Nonsense," he said, "Jane's happy enough.
What could she want better? A good home, a
chance to travel sometimes, — and I'm sure we
are all fond of Janey. No, no, she's happy
enough. Besides, she might not have found a
good husband."

And Mrs. Temple assented, with a sigh of
thankfulness for her own blessings.

III.

Miss Jane thought very often of Mr. Tommy's sorrow. She saw him once or twice in the
village after that walk home from prayer-meeting, and she met him again in the west pasture,
where she had gone to look for wild strawberries
for her sister-in-law, a task which could not be
entrusted to the dull eyes of servants, — and
Dick was too busy, and Effie did not like the
July sun even as late as five o'clock.

Miss Jane had stopped in the pasture to rest
upon a ledge of rock, which, breaking through

the hillside grass and ferns, was grasped by the
roots of a walnut-tree, wrinkled like fingers of
a sinewy hand. She liked to hear the rustle
of the wind in the sage-bush at her side, and
the shrill cry of the crickets. She took off her
hat and smoothed back a lock of her pale brown
hair; then she watched a wandering butterfly
light upon a swinging stalk of mullein, and open
and close his velvety wings. She was wondering, her eyes fixed absently upon the butterfly,
if it would be very long before her brother
opened the old house again, or whether she could
not persuade her sister-in-law to persuade him
to come next summer, — this country life was
very dear to Jane Temple, — so she did not hear
Mr. Tommy's step, and his voice startled her
when he said timidly, "Good-evening, ma'am."
But she was distinctly glad to see him. He
was part of Old Chester to Jane Temple. The
apothecary's arms were full of pennyroyal, and
as he talked he buried his face in it once or
twice, as though its fragrance delighted him,
though really it was only to hide his embarrassed joy.

"I've been picking pennyroyal," he said, as
if its aromatic perfume needed any explanation; "it grows very thickly on the Common."
Then, a little awkwardly, he pulled out half a
dozen sprays from his bunch, and offered them
to Miss Jane. "Some like it," he observed.

"I do," she answered; and from that it was easy enough to fall to talking of his garden, and how dear Old Chester was to Miss Jane, and how sorry she should be when November came, and she must leave it — "And it may be very long before we come back again," she ended, with a sigh.

They were both so interested that they had not noticed how the shadows had lengthened, and then faded into the gray, warm dusk; but when they did, Miss Jane rose nervously.

"Dear me," she said, "how late it is! I must make haste."

Tommy stumbled along at her side over the uneven ground, trying to see the path through his great bunch of pennyroyal. "Miss Jane," he said, a little breathless as he tried to keep pace with her, "if — if you 'll let me, I 'll bring you a bunch of those gillyflowers I told you about."

"Why, indeed, I shall be very glad to have them," she answered. "You are so kind. But I 'm afraid it will be a trouble, Mr. Dove."

These little talks with the apothecary had lent him a new dignity in Miss Jane's eyes, and she no longer called him "Mr. Tommy."

"Why," he protested, "why, it will be the greatest pleasure in the world, the greatest pleasure in the world!"

He walked to Henry Temple's gate with her, and then stood peering between the iron bars at her small figure hurrying along the driveway under the overhanging trees.

Miss Jane was late, and she came breathlessly into the dining-room, to find the family at tea.

"Well, Janey," said her brother, "we began to think you were going to spend the night in the fields ! "

"I am so sorry," she answered, with anxious contrition. "I really did n't know how late it was. Have you tried to make the tea, dear sister? Do let me take your place. I 'm sure you are tired, and — I 'm *so* sorry ! "

"But what happened to you, Janey?" Mr. Temple asked good-naturedly; he had finished his curry, and could afford to be interested in small matters. "I suppose you have brought home a bushel of strawberries?"

"No, she has n't ! " cried Effie shrilly, from her perch on Dick's knee. "She has n't been picking strawberries all this time. I went out to meet her, so I did, an' I got to the pasture bars, an' then I did n't go any farther, 'cause I saw aunty sitting under the big walnut with Mr. Tommy Dove, — an' I don't like that Mr. Tommy Dove."

"What?" exclaimed Henry Temple, his eyes full of amusement. "Does the apothecary go strawberrying, too?"

"Aunty, I'll get the strawberries for you, next time!" said Dick, with a laugh.

Miss Jane tried to make herself heard. "I — I was just going to say, dear brother" — she began, her anxious face hot with blushes — "I met Mr. Dove; he came across the pasture, and I was resting — and he" —

"Yes, yes, we understand," said Mr. Temple, pushing his chair back. "Euphemia, I think Jane will prefer that Effie is kept at home in the afternoons. Effie, confine yourself to large facts, my child: say you went to meet your aunt, but spare the details. Eh, Jane?"

His jolly laugh drowned her answer, and he did not wait for her to repeat it; indeed, the whole matter went out of his mind, nor did it occur to him again until a week later, when Mrs. Temple, with a droll look, told him that Mr. Tommy had brought Miss Jane a bunch of gillyflowers, and had stayed talking with her upon the porch for nearly an hour.

"Well, now, see here," he said, as he flung his head back, with a great laugh. "It is absurd, of course, but really Jane must be careful. It is all very well to be kind and neighborly, — nobody believes in that sort of thing more than I do; only it must not be turned into Love's Offering, Euphemia!" He was even careful to drop a good-natured sarcasm concerning Mr.

Tommy in Miss Jane's presence, and had a moment of uncomfortable surprise at seeing his sister's face flush a little. But, after all, Jane was a woman and a Temple, and was but properly kind-hearted; and then, beside, the little man knew his place.

To take the small bunch of flowers to Miss Jane had been a great pleasure to Mr. Tommy. He thought of it so continuously that he was strangely absent-minded when he mixed his powders and potions, thereby causing. no little anxiety to some nervous customers. He began to say to himself that Miss Jane had received his little nosegay with such kindness that he wished he had something better to give her. After meditating for several days upon this subject, it occurred to him that there was a certain blue chest in the garret which held women's gowns and some small fineries of his mother's. Yet it was not until he had once more walked home from prayer-meeting with her that he made up his mind to open it, and see if it contained anything worthy of Henry Temple's sister.

The Dove house was full of the slumberous silence of the August afternoon, when Tommy climbed the dusty stairs to search the blue chest. The garret under the roof was very hot, and there was a scorched smell from the worm-eaten rafters that mingled with the pungent fragrance of herbs which were drying upon the floor. A blue fly buzzed fitfully up and down one of the small panes of glass in the window, and the hot silence was accented by the tick of the death-watch in the wall, or the muffled stir of bird life under the eaves outside. Against the brick chimney, which was rough with lines of mortar, were spider's-webs, furry with the dust of years; and in a tarnished brass warming-pan was a family of mice, that started at Tommy's step, the mother peering at him with bright, anxious eyes, and then running across the floor to hide beneath a loosened plank.

Tommy propped the window open with a broken sandal - wood box, which held nothing more valuable than some old yellow letters; the blue fly spread his wings and tumbled out into the sunshine, and the fresh air came in, in a warm, sweet gust. Then he lifted the lid of the chest and looked in. There was a vague regret for himself in Tommy's mind, that the contents roused no sacred sorrow; indeed, he was much more conscious of what a refuge the garret had been to him in his boyhood, when he longed to escape from the sharp, scolding voice to which he never dared reply; but he forgot this as he lifted out two gowns and examined them critically. One was of shimmering gray, with small bunches of purple flowers scattered

over it, and the other of thin changeable silk.
He held them out at arm's-length and reflected.
. They did not seem quite like the dresses Miss
Jane wore, but he could not tell why. Then a
thought struck him. He looked towards the
door by which he had entered, and though he
knew that in the empty house there were no
other curious eyes than those of the gray mouse,
he stepped back across the uneven floor, and
shut and bolted the door. There was a mirror
in one corner, hanging high upon the discolored
wall; its worn gilt frame flung a shadow on its
powdery surface, but Mr. Tommy, standing on
tiptoe, and holding the gray dress up in front
of him, could catch a glimpse of the high waist
and balloon sleeves. He shook his head: the
dresses would not do, he thought; they did not
look like Miss Jane. He laid the gowns down
upon a cowhide trunk, upon the cover of which
" Dove " was marked in brass nailheads, and
began his search again.

There was not much to hope for among the
bonnets and chintz gowns and queer mantillas,
but almost at the bottom of the chest he found
a square package folded in silvered paper. This
he opened anxiously. It contained a pale pea-
green crêpe shawl, embroidered along the edge,
and with heavy silk fringe laid straight and
smooth. Tommy breathed quick with pleasure.

He could not have explained it, but this seemed as though it belonged to Miss Jane. He replaced the other things, and then closed the lid of the chest and sat down upon it.

He shook the shawl out of its folds of forty years, and held it up to dusk and gleam in the sunshine. Yes, it was certainly beautiful, and it was the very thing for Miss Jane. But how should he give it to her? Was it best to wrap it up again and send it to her; or had he better throw it over his arm, and walk up the hill, and just remark — incidentally — something about shawls? He lifted the silvered paper, that it might help him to decide, but it fell apart along the worn creases. After all, that settled it. He would carry it to her folded across his arm; it would make too much of it to present her with a packet.

He shut the small window, but stopped to turn the pennyroyal over, before he left the old garret to its hot stillness.

The apothecary was not in a position to know that Henry Temple was entertaining some gentlemen at dinner that evening, but it would have spared him some pain could he have guessed it. As it was, he was impatient for the tall clock in the shop to strike eight, that, with the shawl upon his arm, he might walk up the shadowy lane to the white house on the hill.

As Mrs. Temple was too great an invalid to
be present on such occasions, Miss Jane took
the head of her brother's table. She was so
silent and timid a hostess that by degrees Henry
Temple's friends had ceased to feel that politeness made it necessary to try to include her in
their conversation. Miss Jane had no small
feminine opinions upon social or political prob-
lems; she was filled with mild astonishment to
learn that their talk of *der Aberglaube* was a
religious discussion, and she saw no connection
between "Reform" and politics. Indeed, she
rarely knew what they were talking about, and
it was always a relief to her when she was
allowed to leave them to their cigars and wine,
and retire to the parlor. There, on this still
August evening while Tommy was hastening
up the hill, she was sitting, patiently waiting to
give them their coffee. There was a bowl of
roses on the table beside her, and she was trying, by the light of two candles in the twisted
arms of a tall candelabrum, to read one of her
brother's learned books. Miss Jane was con-
stantly "improving her mind." As Tommy
caught a glimpse of her through one of the open
French windows, it seemed to him that there
was a halo round her bending head, such as he
had seen about the gracious faces of pictured
saints.

It was unfortunate that, at that moment, Henry Temple and his guests should have been coming through the hall from the dining-room. It was impossible not to see Tommy's shrinking figure in the doorway, his small face quivering with embarrassment, and the green shawl upon his arm making a spot of white under the porch lamp.

"What does this person want, Jane?" her brother said, in a low, annoyed tone.

"I — I must ask you to excuse me, brother," she answered, frightened, yet with the loyalty of a gentle heart. "I think Mr. Dove has come to see — me; so will you please let John pour out the coffee?"

Henry Temple frowned. "Very well," he said briefly; and then he joined again in the drawing-room conversation of the men, explaining with good-natured carelessness that they must take their coffee by themselves.

The apothecary followed Miss Jane to the library, but he would not sit down; he stood first on one foot, and then on the other, nervously rolling the shawl into a muff to hide his hands. "I'll go right home again, ma'am," he said. "I won't interrupt you — I won't stay."

"Oh, please don't go, Mr. Dove," Miss Jane remonstrated tremulously. "My brother is —

is occupied, but I'll be glad if you will stay and talk to me."

So Tommy stayed a little while. Once, when Henry Temple came in to find some book, he rose, and said, "Good-evening, sir," with respectful timidity. Mr. Temple's good nature was restored by that time, and he answered, "Oh, how are you, Tommy?" in a way which warmed the apothecary's heart. He did not stay long after that; but when he rose to go, it took some little time to find suitable language in which to present his gift to Miss Jane. He stumbled over his words as he tried to tell her that he hoped she would accept it. "If you will please to take it," he ended, holding the shawl out to her entreatingly.

Miss Jane was as confused as he. "Indeed, Mr. Dove" — she protested.

"It was my — my dear mother's," he said imploringly. "I'd like to think you were wearing it. There never was anybody else I could have given it to, — except Mary Ellen Boyce, and mother didn't like her, — and if — if you would just be willing" —

"Why," said Miss Jane, the tears coming into her eyes with embarrassed pleasure, "I hardly know how to refuse, you are so kind, and it is so beautiful; only I — I ought not to accept it, you know."

"Oh, please do. ma'am!" burst out Tommy.

And Miss Jane could only take it, touching it with her white fingers in womanly enjoyment of its exquisite texture. "Why, it's as fine as a cobweb," she said. "You are too kind, Mr. Dove."

Tommy went home thrilled with happiness. Miss Jane thought him "kind;" she had taken his little present, and said it was "beautiful"! The very existence of Mary Ellen Boyce faded out of his mind; his heart beat high with pride; he said to himself that he really did not know what he should do when Miss Jane went away from Old Chester.

Perhaps that was the moment when a vague, undefined thought first came into the apothecary's mind. *Perhaps she need not go away?* Tommy was actually frightened at himself. "Why," he said aloud, "if Miss Jane knew I had thought of such a thing, she would be very angry with me."

Then the image of Henry Temple presented itself, and Tommy shivered. Nevertheless, with a sort of awful pleasure, he said again, "Perhaps she need not go away!"

IV.

That was the first of half a dozen calls. Miss Jane began not only to enjoy them, but to look forward to them. It was impossible not to be touched by the subtle flattery of Tommy's timidity, and, following that, his honest belief in her judgment which dared to be admiration; but yet more flattering was the simplicity with which he showed his happiness if he could but be near her. It brought a new pleasure into Miss Jane's life; a pleasure which was, perhaps, greater because her brother had been called away from home for a few weeks, and she did not fear his sarcasms. The amused and annoyed looks of Mrs. Temple and Dick hurt her only when she saw them; she began to feel a certain bravery for her own life which she had never known before. Dearly as she loved these dear people, and absorbed as she was in their interests, she began to see that it was possible that she might have an interest which should be all her own, and to realize that there was room in the life which they had seemed to fill for an affection which did not need their sanction. She was conscious of a feeling of proprietorship; a new and trembling dignity crept into her manner. To be sure, it could be overthrown by a word. Effie's remark that the green crêpe shawl, which, one evening, she boldly threw across her shoulders, was "a hideous old thing," made her quick to put it away; but there were some rose-geranium leaves from one of Tommy's nosegays between its soft folds. The alteration in her manner was so slight, however, that Henry Temple, at least, would never have noticed it, or been particularly concerned that the apothecary should call, had not Tommy's first visit after his return fallen upon an evening when her brother needed Miss Jane's services.

"Really, Euphemia," he said, on finding that Jane had been summoned to the parlor to see Mr. Dove, "isn't this thing getting to be something more serious than a bore?"

Mr. Temple was standing with his back to the fire, one elbow on the mantelshelf behind him, and a cigar between his fingers. His handsome face showed decided annoyance. "I wanted Jane to copy some manuscript for me, and here comes this confounded apothecary to delay me. What business has the fellow to be here, anyhow? What is Jane thinking of to allow it?"

As Mr. Temple reflected upon his inconvenience, his irritation increased.

"It's clear enough what Tommy's thinking of," said Dick, who was lounging about the room, with his hands in his pockets: "he's in love

with aunty. The romance of the apothecary is
a perfect nuisance in this household. I wanted
her to mend my cap for me to-night. Effie, you
humbug, why don't you learn to sew and mend
your brother's things?"

" 'Cause," Effie replied concisely; and then
she added, "I met him in the village yesterday, that Mr. Tommy Dove, an' he asked me if
aunty was going to be at home last night, an'
I told him no, she was n't."

"But, Effie, dear," protested her mother from
the sofa, "she *was* at home."

"I know it," said Effie calmly, "but I did n't
want him round. I wanted her to play back-
gammon with me, so I did n't want him round."

Mrs. Temple's troubled remonstrance was
drowned in her husband's rollicking laugh.

"Well done, Ef!" he said; "but the ecclesi-
astical game should teach you a regard for truth
— though, on the whole, no; it would have the
opposite effect, of course. Don't play it, child,
its influence upon your morals is so evident.
But, seriously, Euphemia — Go to bed, Effie,
and remember, I will not allow untruthfulness;"
and when she had gone pouting upstairs, for a
punishment which it chanced to be convenient
to her father to administer, — for the child's
presence was a restraint in a conversation of this
nature, — he finished his sentence: "I don't like

this at all. Has this person been coming here
to see Jane?"

"Yes, he has," said Dick, who was sitting
on the arm of his mother's sofa, and examining
the loop of his hunting-crop critically. "It's
perfectly ridiculous. Something ought to be
done."

"Oh, Richard, dear," said his mother, in her
weak voice, "don't say such a thing to your
father. It is nothing, my dear; he has called
occasionally, but I've no doubt it has only been
about — about my medicine."

"Nonsense," said her husband briefly, with
an annoyed glance at the clock. "I won't get
that manuscript off in the morning. Dick, just
tell me how long this thing has been going on,
will you?"

"Well," Dick answered, "he has been coming once a week, certainly. In fact, I think
this is the second time this week. Mother,
darling, you must take a good deal of medicine?"

"But there's no harm, Henry," Mrs. Temple
said anxiously. "Sometimes I think we are almost selfish about Janey. We expect her to be
satisfied to have only *our* pleasures, not her own."

"Now, Euphemia," Mr. Temple answered,
gesticulating with his half-smoked cigar, "you
really must not be absurd, you know. I'm per-

fectly willing for Jane to have her own pleasures
when they are reasonable and proper. But I
don't propose to receive the apothecary at my
house to divert Jane Temple, — granted it is
only diversion, and nothing more serious. But
I'm inclined to think it is more serious. Do
you want Tommy for a brother - in - law, my
dear?"

"If Janey were fond of him" — Mrs. Temple
began, trembling.

"Euphemia," interrupted her husband, "you
have heard me remark, I think, that I hate a
fool; now try and understand, please, that I am
only anxious for Jane's best happiness. There's
nobody more anxious for her happiness than I
am. But do you suppose she could be happy
with such a person as this Tommy Dove?
Pshaw! It isn't to be considered seriously,
— it is preposterous!"

He flung his cigar down on the smouldering
logs with an angry exclamation.

"Your father will have his joke," Mrs. Temple said, looking at her son with wistful apology for her husband. "Of course, dear, I know
you only do what is best for us all. No doubt
it would be a great mistake for Janey; I only
thought" —

"Don't think!" interrupted Henry Temple
with a laugh; "it is one of the greatest mis-

takes. Never think; and don't argue about things, my dear, — just accept them. That is what I am going to do now, and end this folly."

"And what aunty will do," Dick said, — "she 'll accept the apothecary."

"I think not," returned his father grimly.

All this time, Mr. Tommy, unusually nervous, but very happy, was sitting in the chilly parlor with Miss Jane. He had come to Henry Temple's house that night with a purpose. He knew that Miss Jane would very soon go away from Old Chester, perhaps not to return for years; and unless he could persuade her to stay, who could tell whether he might ever see her again? And though he trembled at his own presumption, he meant to try to persuade her. He had dreamed of this moment for weeks; every word to her had been uttered with the distinct intention of encouraging himself; every look had betrayed his thought.

Mr. Tommy had felt vaguely that the atmosphere of the place was against him. Yet Effie was the embodiment of its antagonism, he thought, rather than the master of the house, and so of late he had, in many humble little ways, tried to propitiate the child. He had gathered small nosegays, and, tying a bit of bright ribbon about them with awkward fingers, had offered them to Miss Jane, with the request

that she would give them to "the little girl."
He never knew that, though she thanked him,
and told him he "was so kind to remember
Effie," the flowers went no further than Miss
Jane's own dressing-table. Nor did a game,
which he had purchased in the village, fare any
better; nor a picture of a girl and a dog. But
as Mr. Tommy never guessed the gentle fate of
his gifts, he was not discouraged, and so continued to offer them, with unabated hope that
the contemptuous Effie would soon dislike him
less.

On this sharp October night, he brought in
the pocket of his black coat six little red-cheeked
apples. He had polished them stealthily upon
his sleeve as he climbed the hill, and when he
laid them in a row upon the table, in front of
Miss Jane, they actually shone in the lamplight.

"They are paradise apples," he said, "and I
brought them for the little girl. I thought may
be she would like them."

Miss Jane was very nervous that evening;
perhaps she had guessed the intention of the
apothecary's call; at all events, her mild face
was full of anxious indecision, though she was
strangely happy.

"Indeed, you are too good, Mr. Dove," she
said; she had hurried upstairs for the green
shawl, when he had been announced, and she

drew it now a little closer about her shoulders;
"Those paradise apples are so pretty."

"They are rather sour," Tommy answered
doubtfully, "but they seemed pretty, and I
thought the little girl might like to play with
them."

"We had one of those trees in the lower garden, when I was a child," said Miss Jane, "but
it is dead now; the garden has run wild in all
these years we have been away. I wish brother
could live here, and it could be taken care of,
and look as it used to."

"Do you?" Tommy said slowly. He was
not particularly anxious that Mr. Henry Temple should remain in Old Chester.

"Yes," she responded; "but I suppose it
would be too lonely in the winter."

The apothecary hastened to agree with her in
this, and to tell her how desolate the great house
looked in winter, when the snow drifted across
the porch, or lay unbroken on the window ledges
and the thresholds. "The house is so high on
the hill, ma'am," he explained, "that the wind
just sweeps it all the time. But it's pleasanter
in the valley, Miss Jane."

Then they talked of Old Chester as it was
long ago, and Miss Jane reminded him of the
coast on the Common. "The gypsies used to
camp there in the summer, — do you remem-

ber? — but in the winter we children used to go
sledding. I had a blue sled, and Billy Spear
— he was our coachman — used to pull it up
the hill for me."

Mr. Tommy listened ecstatically, the palms
of his lean hands squeezed together between his
knees. "Yes, yes," he said; "oh, dear me,
yes, indeed, it *was* pleasant! If you were
going to be here in the winter again, ma'am,
I — I could pull the blue sled up the hill for
you, Miss Jane."

"Oh," replied Miss Jane sadly, without the
slightest consciousness of humor, "it 's broken
now; the children broke it. And your rheumatism, Mr. Dove? "

"But I would n't mind that," cried Tommy,
— "oh, my, no ! Oh, Miss Jane, if you — only
could — stay ! "

"But I could n't, you know, Mr. Dove," she
answered, the color coming and going in her
faded cheek, and her voice unsteady. "I
could n't let brother's family go back without
me, and I could not be here alone, of course.
But I shall miss — Old Chester."

She seemed to crouch further back into her
chair, but Tommy sat quite upon the edge of
his. Their two hearts beat so quickly that they
were both a little breathless as they spoke.

"But," said Mr. Tommy, huskily, rubbing

his hands together and edging yet farther forward, "if I — I mean if you — if we — if it could be arranged; — if — if — Oh, *don't* you understand, ma'am?"

"Oh, no, indeed, I don't," said Miss Jane faintly; "not at all, I'm sure. And it couldn't — could it?"

"Oh, my goodness, Miss Jane," said Tommy, almost crying, "I'll — I'll do anything — if you — if you just will" —

Here the door opened, and Henry Temple walked leisurely into the room.

"Ah, — Jane," he said, looking with calm directness at Tommy, yet without the slightest sign that he saw him, though the apothecary had risen and bowed, and bowed again. "There is some manuscript on my table which I wish you would be so kind as to copy for me."

"Yes, brother," she said, white and trembling, "I will. But — Mr. Dove — you didn't see that Mr. Dove is here."

"Oh," returned Mr. Temple, gazing quite blankly at Tommy's quivering little face, while he fumbled for his glasses. He adjusted them, and his dark eyebrows gathered in a fleeting frown. "Ah, Tommy? Good-evening, Tommy. You will excuse Miss Temple, I am sure. Jane, be good enough to attend to that, if you please."

He stood holding the door open and looking

down at Tommy with a high, calm glance which burned into the apothecary's soul.

"Brother!" Jane cried, her voice unsteady with anger. Yet she did not finish her sentence. Mr. Tommy interrupted her.

"Oh, yes," he said, — "oh, dear me — why, certainly — yes. I'm just going, just going!" He seemed to shrink and grow smaller, as he slipped sideways past Henry Temple and sought blindly for his hat in the hall. "Yes, yes," he repeated. "Good-night, sir, good-night." He did not even look at Miss Jane, but opened the front door, and, stumbling with haste, without stopping for his lantern which he had left at the foot of the steps, he found his way under the heavy shadows of the trees to the gate.

The sharp, cold wind seemed to brush the mist of his preposterous dream aside. He closed the iron gate with a clang behind him, and ran with all his might down the stony lane, his little legs shaking under him, and his eyes stinging with tears.

"Oh, — *my!*" he said to himself. There was a lump in his throat, and he almost sobbed aloud.

That next hour in Jane Temple's unselfish life left its lasting imprint on her gentle face. She had followed her brother into the library, and, trembling in every limb, and with frightened eyes, listened to Henry Temple's announcement that he meant to put a stop to this folly.

"You don't understand these things, Jane," he said, "and it's my duty to protect you from the consequences of your ignorance. I'm always kind to the poor people about here, — I make a point of it; they are well meaning and inoffensive, — but kindness from a woman in your position to such a person as this apothecary will be misunderstood. He will begin to imagine he is in love with you."

"He's making a fool of himself," Dick broke in. "Somebody ought to do something about it. He's trespassing upon your good-nature, aunty."

"Dick," said Miss Jane, holding her head high, "I will listen to anything your father says, because he is my brother, and he has a right to speak, but I will not hear you say such things. Mr. Dove is — my friend. I will not listen to you."

There was a moment of astonished silence; then, at a look from his father, Dick muttered an apology. But Henry Temple, with a calm indifference which might almost have been mistaken for kindness, added one or two keen, stern words, and then turned to leave the room. He had forgotten the haste about his manu-

script, and, as there was no reason why he
should have the discomfort of seeing his sister's
pain, he preferred to go away.

But he stopped in the doorway, his hands in
his pockets, and looked back at Miss Jane. "I
have no fear that you will forget yourself, Jane,"
he said. "Do not imagine for a moment that I
distrust you, — or your taste. It is mere consideration for poor little Tommy that makes me
speak."

When he had gone, and Dick, with an odd
sensation of shame, had followed him, Mrs.
Temple covered her face with her thin hands
and burst into tears.

"Oh, Janey, you wouldn't leave us ? You
couldn't! I — I'm no use, and Henry depends
so on you he wouldn't have any comfort without you, and — oh, we couldn't get along without you. Of course " — sobbing — "Henry
speaks only for your best happiness. He said
so. For you wouldn't be happy here with Mr.
— Mr. Dove; and that's Henry's first consideration, of course."

Jane Temple's anger melted under those tears.
The old love asserted itself in her faithful heart.
"They *need* me," she thought tenderly. But
though she comforted her sister-in-law with gentle words, the pain remained, and kept the tears
stinging in her eyes, and stirred her into a piti-

ful passion of belief that her own life "had a claim." But when at last, hurt and exhausted and full of uncertainty, she locked herself into her own room, she was vaguely happy. Her eyes filled with gentler tears, and her lips smiled; and when she knelt down to say her prayers, and prayed that she might be submissive and patient, she buried her tear-stained face in the green shawl, and thanked God that Mr. Dove loved her! All that night she tried to see her duty, to conquer her selfishness. But she could not help remembering that she must be just to the apothecary, and that she had some right to her own life; and then the habit of unselfishness brought the first petition to her lips again: "*help me to do my duty!*" She longed for day to come that she might hear the rest of Mr. Tommy's sentence, and comfort her heart with his honest love. "But I must tell him it can never be," she made herself say.

V.

Not since that solemn day when Mrs. Dove had been carried over the threshold of the unused front door had Tommy crossed it; but some instinct which he could not have defined made the apothecary, breathless with his run down the hill, brush the cobwebs away from the key-

hole, and fumble over his bunch of keys, that
he might enter now.

He struck a match in the darkness of the hall,
and, curving his lean hand about it, mounted
the stairs to the parlor above the shop. On the
mantelpiece, in the head of a dusty china shepherdess, was a candle, bent sideways by the
summer's heats. This he lighted and put upon
the centre-table.

The parlor had the musty smell of a long-
closed room, and as he touched the table he felt
the grit of dust. He sat down upon the slippery
horsehair sofa, and buried his face in his hands.
The candle flickered a little in the current of air
from the open door, and cast upon the wall a
grotesque shadow of his bending head; a drop of
wax fell with a white splash upon the rosewood
table. Tommy raised his head, and looked about
the dreary room. He did not spare himself one
detail of its ugliness.

The furniture was stiff and clumsy. There
were engravings upon the walls of celebrated
persons in their libraries, and a print of Henry
Clay's deathbed, suitably framed in a wiry
imitation of crape. A yellowing cast of little
Samuel knelt in one corner, and some faded
family photographs of not attractive people
hung in a row high above the black mantel, on
which was a large conch shell, whose curving

red lip held a bunch of dried grass and certain silky white seed-pods. There was a silent clock upon the mantel, too, with a bell-glass over it, and a bunch of wax flowers in a blue vase; and on a fuzzy green mat upon a side table were the family Bible and the large parlor lamp with its knitted shade.

Mr. Tommy's haggard eyes traveled slowly from point to point. How had he dared to dream that he might ask Henry Temple's sister to come to such a home! But oh, how, in this last month, his life had been brightened by the mere thought of such a thing! Tommy squeezed his hands together and groaned; but it was because of his intolerable humiliation rather than his despair, for now Miss Jane seemed such worlds away from him that he did not realize he had ever hoped. His whole lean body tingled with mortification. He pressed his fingers hard upon his eyes, and his breath came fast.

The candle burned down to the head of the china shepherdess, guttered, smoked, and, wavering into a sickly blue flame, went out. The darkness of the long-closed room seemed palpable as it closed about him; but before his eyes was still the glimmer of the lamps in Mr. Temple's drawing-room, and the silence of the empty house was jarred by that insolently courteous voice.

By and by there was a faint lightening of the heavy darkness; through the round hole in the closed wooden shutter came the gray gleam of dawn. It touched the motionless figure on the old sofa, and little by little the furniture began to take vague shapes in the shadows. Tommy lifted his head, and watched the daylight creep stealthily about.

At last he rose, slowly and stiffly, and went to the window and tried to push the shutter back. The ivy held it outside, and the hinges were rusty, but it yielded a little, and then opened half way. A white mist shut out the hills, and a stone's-throw from the gate the road was swallowed up in it.

The cold air struck his face like a rebuff from the great world outside; he shivered as he closed and bolted the shutter. He looked to see that he had left no matches about, and that there was no spark smouldering in the china shepherdess; then he crept silently out of the room.

Mr. Tommy Dove had made up his mind.

First he wrote a line to Mrs. McDonald, and pinned it to the white curtain in the kitchen window; then he went upstairs to the garret. There was a traveling-bag there, he thought. He groped in the dark corner under the mirror until he laid his hand upon it. As he left the room he caught sight of the blue chest, and his

sudden pang of regret was like physical pain.
He took the shabby bag to his room, and with
unsteady hands thrust a few of his possessions
into it. His money he put into his breast-
pocket, and then looked at himself in the glass
to see if any one could guess that under his
tightly buttoned coat lay his little store of
wealth. Some loose change he dropped into a
snuff-box, which it was his custom to use instead
of a purse, and as he did so he noticed one new,
shining penny. The habit of these last weeks
asserted itself, and he thought of Effie; but it
was only for a moment.

A little later, Mr. Tommy Dove opened his
shop door and let himself out into the dawn.

In the thick mist that covered the garden, the
frosted flower-stalks stood up like brown, thin
ghosts, and there was a heavy scent of wet fallen
leaves. Mr. Tommy peered anxiously about
for a last pansy, or for some belated sweet pea
that had not yet taken wing; but he could find
only two small, dull asters, and a wilted spray
of salvia rimmed with frosted dew. These he
picked, tying them together with a long, wet
blade of grass. He looked back once at the old
stone house; the reddening ivy on the south wall
was thinned by frost, and was shining faintly,
as though it had rained in the night. The
damp horse - chestnut leaves that covered the

ground like a yellow mantle hardly rustled as
he walked through them to the road.

It did not take Mr. Tommy very long to
climb the lane to Henry Temple's gate. He
did not enter, but stood pressing his face against
the wet, cold iron, and staring up the dim driveway.

"Oh, dear me!" he said, with a catch in his
breath. "Why, just think of it, I'll never see
her again; and the only thing in the world I
can do for her is just to go away!"

Then, with a dull ache in his heart, he began
to say to himself that he knew what a relief it
would be to Miss Jane not to see him.

"She has such a tender heart," he said; "she
would be so sorry to make me feel badly by saying 'no.' Oh my, to think I ever supposed
she'd say anything else! It seems so selfish in
me, but — but I did."

He looked at the bunch of wilted flowers,
and touched them softly with reverent fingers.
A moment later he laid them down against the
stone gatepost, and then went slowly back into
the mist.

. . . .

Miss Jane Temple, still irresolute, still miserable, but yet strangely happy, waited for Mr.
Tommy all that dim October day. She did not
hear until nearly a week later, a week of mis-

givings and grief and wounded pride, that the shop in the village was closed, and that no one knew just where the apothecary had gone nor when he would return. She never saw the asters and the salvia; and the great iron gate, swinging open to let her go away from her old home, told her no story.

"After all," Mrs. Temple comforted herself, when the family were safe in town again, "we need n't have been anxious. He never could have dreamed of such a thing, though Henry thought he did, — and so did Janey! But an unmarried woman of her age is very likely to make such a mistake."

THE FACE ON THE WALL.

I.

"But what does she see in him to love?"

"Well, she sees something, evidently; and if Annie sees it, that is all that is necessary."

"Oh, yes, yes; I know. But if he would only show us some of the good things — I want to like him, I 'm sure."

Annie Murray had been married that morning, and now, in the early December dusk, her four sisters, tired by the excitement of the day, quivering yet from the pain of parting, sat by the fire in the parlor talking it all over. They had said to one another how pretty she was, how nicely her gray traveling dress fitted, and how well their mother's pearl pin looked in the lace about her throat; and then Miss Sarah Murray, the eldest of the five sisters, said, with an effort that brought the blood into her delicate old face, "And — and Mr. Calkins; he appeared very well, I thought."

No one spoke for a moment. The repression which they had put upon themselves after Annie had finally, despairingly, set their pleadings aside and engaged herself to Paul Calkins, that repression still commanded them.

"Oh, yes, he appeared very well," Mary said vaguely. And then there was silence for the space of a breath, till Miss Nannie broke out with the cry of "What *does* she see in him to love?" To hear their own thought put into words startled these four gentle, kindly women like a thread of electricity leaping around their circle by the fireside.

Annie was their youngest; and yet not so young that she had not caught a little of their sweet precision, their soft, reserved femininity. The people in Mercer who knew the Murrays, and were of a younger and more irreverent age, called them the five old maids; but their friends of a more courteous generation always spoke of them as the "Murray girls," though Miss Sarah was at least fifty-five, and Mary, next in youth to Annie, was over forty. No one dreamed that any of the Murray girls would marry; no one ever had dreamed of such a thing since the time when Edward Paul jilted Miss Sarah for a cleverer woman, who dazzled his eyes and blinded him, even as the flare of a candle may sometimes hide a star. Annie was a baby when Sarah Murray's grief came to her, — a grief which touched her life like a consecrating hand, putting her quietly back from happiness into usefulness. She devoted herself to her sisters; especially to Annie, to whom she gave that mother-love which childless women know. Annie was nearly thirty years younger than Sarah, but she too was a "Murray girl;" quiet, old-fashioned, — old-maidish, the irreverent said. So when, at last, suddenly, Annie had a lover, people looked a little blank, and said: "What? Annie Murray? Why, we never supposed" — And then they had to adjust their idea of the five sisters, and observe that Annie at twenty-seven, a little prim, with sweet, delicate, old-fashioned ways, was yet an exceedingly pretty woman, full of the calm attraction of pleasant silence. They began to say that Annie was so quiet that they had never known her. "That youngest Murray girl is like a handful of rose leaves," somebody said; "but I believe she has more to her than any of the others." And then all her little world began to take the greatest interest in her wooing.

Somehow, in spite of their reserve, it came out that the four older sisters were opposed to the match. Perhaps their disapproval was guessed by the trouble in Annie's eyes, or the servants' tattle betrayed it, or people may have seen for themselves — and then drawn their own conclusions — the coarse, weak lines in Paul's face; a face which made the pathetic confession that the poor soul behind it, agonize as it might, was dogged and hunted by the body, dominated by the flesh.

But there was one other way in which the sisters' disapproval had been made known: Mr. Calkins had been willing to laugh a little, good-naturedly, at the "four old maids who were afraid of him."

"That he could speak of such matters, Annie dear, that he could tell anybody that we were not pleased — don't you see? It shows that he does not have the delicacy that — that we might wish," Miss Sarah had said to her youngest sister.

"You don't understand, Sarah," Annie answered sadly. She never tried by insistence to make them appreciate him; perhaps she was too sensitive for his dignity to take such means; perhaps she realized the worthlessness of regard gained by insistence.

Miss Sarah and the other three alarmed and disapproving women said all they could, prayed for her, agonized over her, cowered at the threat of the future, and then, when at last, in spite of all, Annie Murray gave her word, then they were silent, even to each other, — silent save when, with the fine deceit of love, they applauded to their little world their sister's choice.

Now, however, when it was all over, and she had married him and gone away, and the four bereaved women sat here alone before the parlor fire, Miss Nannie's grief spoke: "What does she see in him?"

"His painting attracts her," Emily said, weakly. And then they all four glanced up at the picture above the fireplace: it had been Paul Calkins's present to his sisters-in-law.

It was a woman's face pressing itself through crowding vine leaves, as though a girl in a vineyard looked for a moment out upon the world: a dim face, with smiling lips and eyes deep with pain, but a pain that had nothing spiritual in it; a beautiful face, yet full of the bitterness that lies behind sensuality.

"Her soul is trying to speak, but it cannot," Annie Murray said, when the sisters stood looking at the canvas, embarrassed at a gift which was kindly meant, but which was not, Miss Nannie said, "pleasing."

Miss Sarah adjusted her glasses twice, pathetically anxious to see what Annie saw. Emily blushed and turned away, for the bare bosom offended her, "and she has too red a lip to be nice," Miss Emily thought. Annie looked at it until a mist shut it out, and then she turned and said something to her lover which the sisters could not hear, but which made the tears

start in his eyes, while he caught her in his arms
and kissed her; which was, Miss Emily said to
herself, "most uncalled for."

Now, to-night, when Annie, as Paul's wife,
was whirling out into the great world, whirling
away from all the love which had protected her
youth, the four sisters looked up at the painted
face, and one sighed, and another shook her
head, and dear Miss Nannie broke down and
cried.

"And his *name*," she said, with a sob, —
"Calkins! Sister, really, a man with a name
like that can't be — can't be" —

"Paul is a good name, Nannie." Miss Sarah
tried to comfort her.

"And we don't know anything about his people!"

"His father and mother are dead," Emily
cautioned her: "we ought not to speak disre-
spectfully of his parents."

"I didn't mean to," Nannie answered, wip-
ing her eyes; "only, Emily, Calkins is a shocking name; and he told me himself that he has
a brother who is a mechanic. Just think how
father would feel!"

"Now, Nannie, Nannie," interposed the old-
est sister, "that is very wrong. I am surprised
at you, my dear. I'm sure, if he will make
Annie happy, I don't care what his brother is.

I only wish I could see the amiable qualities that Annie does, and that I didn't have just a little misgiving at his fondness for — his glass," Miss Sarah ended delicately.

"Annie feels," Emily hastened to explain, "that his living alone so much has encouraged bachelor habits. I believe gentlemen living alone are fond of their glass at dinner. I hope Annie will induce him to drink milk. It is so much more nourishing."

There was no answer save Miss Sarah's sigh; the firelight lapsed and then leaped up, summoning shadows into outline against the dusk, and showing the dignified, comfortable room, which, to the sisters' eyes, was full of suggestions of Annie. There was the old-fashioned square piano, bought just after the war, when the Murrays had more money than in these days of falling interest; Annie had played her little tunes upon it in the summer twilights and winter evenings, ever since Mary had given her her first music lessons, nearly twenty years ago now. The little prim water-color sketches hanging between the windows were Annie's, made before she knew Paul; after meeting him she painted no more, which was a grief to her sisters, who could not know how joyfully a soul may recognize that the art it has dared to touch is too great to be essayed by anything but greatness. There was a sampler Annie had worked when she was ten, used now as a screen between the sofa and the fire; and near the hearth, the little low chair on which she loved to sit, her chin propped on her hands, staring into the flames. Everything reminded them of her; and most of all, the bunch of white roses in a vase upon the table. She had held them that morning when she was married.

"Oh, if he will only be good to her," Miss Nannie said. "But he is so — strange!"

That was the real trouble, the real fear: Paul was so "strange." That he was an artist, that he painted unpleasant pictures, that he had a vulgar name, even that he was fond of his glass, — these were superficial objections. Below them was a grim and terrifying fact: he was unkind to Annie! He was careless of her feelings; he was not polite to her ("that's where the mechanic comes in," Miss Nannie sighed). He had been so impatient and irritable while they were engaged that more than once the sisters had seen traces of tears on her face; he forgot his appointments with her, and then laughed at her anxiety. He loved her? Oh, of course, of course. At least, he seemed to at times. Certainly, he was not hampered by any reserve or delicacy in expressing his affection — when he felt it. He did not hesitate to kiss

Annie before the sisters, although the four
elderly women blushed hotly, and looked away,
and wondered how Annie could endure "such
things." Still, that was Love, no doubt. But
what sort of love was it that could be unkind?
What weight did it have against rudeness that
once Miss Emily found him on his knees before
Annie, saying hoarsely, "I 'm a brute to you ! "

"You *are!* " Emily said to herself bitterly.
"If it was n't true, there might be some merit
in saying so. You 'd better mend your manners than say how bad they are."

But Annie was apparently so sure of his love
that his manners, which the sisters felt spoke
his character, caused her no concern. Yet how
could love like that insure her happiness?

No wonder that these four women, who also
loved her, sat with heavy hearts about the
hearth on this evening of Annie Murray's wed-
ding-day.

II.

When the letters began to come, there was
nothing to read between the lines. Paul's
work, Paul's plans, Paul's high ideals, — the
four Misses Murray read of these until they
felt, as Miss Nannie said, "as though dear Paul
occupied Annie's thoughts very much."

"Well, that is as it should be," Emily said

sturdily. "I'm sure if she wasn't attached to
him, then we should have cause for anxiety."

And they felt they could conscientiously say
to their friends that Annie was very happy,
even though they themselves were not happy
about her.

Once in the first year Miss Nannie went to
see Annie, and came back looking older, and
with vague, half-frightened perplexity in her
face. "I cannot understand Paul," she told
her sisters: "but I'm sure he means to do
right."

And then, little by little, she confessed her
perplexities: Annie had very little money;
Nannie felt it was fortunate that her own quarter's allowance had scarcely been touched save
for this trip. Annie was a little fussy about
taking it, but Paul told her not to be foolish.
"Paul is very sensible about such things," Nannie said. It did not seem as though they were
living in a pleasant neighborhood; but Annie
explained that by saying that rents were high,
and Paul didn't mind where he lived, he was
so full of his work.

"That shows a good spirit," Emily declared;
and Miss Nannie said, "Yes; oh, of course,"
and sighed; "and yet," she ended, "Paul does
say such — such wrong things to Annie!"

"Does Annie seem happy?" Sarah asked,

putting her sewing down in her lap because her hands trembled.

"Yes," Nannie answered; "but — I don't know why she should be!"

It was nearly a year later that Miss Sarah made her visit; it was then that the baby was born, and died. Annie had grieved, but not as one would think a woman would grieve for her first-born; her only thought seemed to be to get well as soon as possible, for Paul's sake. Her illness and his anxiety about her — which took the form of excessive irritability — interfered with his work: she must get well! As for Paul, it seemed to Miss Sarah that he was quite without natural feeling.

"You are well out of it!" was all he said when, with clear, bright eyes, he stood looking down at the placid mystery of the little dead face. But he stood there a long time. This little creature had stolen out of Annie's love and his, parting like a curtain their consciousnesses, and then turning for a moment on the threshold of death to look back, wise and mocking, before it slipped out into silence.

Perhaps Paul, looking down at the dead child, felt afraid of its little separate existence, — loved it, hated it, wondered at it; wished he could follow it and grasp the mystery; felt, perhaps, half sorry for the unspent life, yet felt, too, the pang of the prisoner who sees freedom granted to some one else. Perhaps he was confronted by his fatherhood, and it came into his mind that with such a father the little quivering, hesitating life, blown out into the darkness, was well rid of living? One cannot tell. The tears were in his eyes, and he turned to Miss Sarah, with a laugh: "This world isn't a good place; the young one is well out of it."

When Miss Sarah went home, she did not attempt any further disguise with herself or her sisters: the marriage had turned out badly. Annie was very poor, for her quarterly allowance was not enough to support two, and Paul's pictures did not seem, Miss Sarah said, "to be popular." "Oh, no doubt he's fond of her — in his way," the older sister admitted with an effort; but he was unkind to her, bitterly neglectful, full of insistent demands upon her time and strength and love. These were the facts, and the four women had to accept them as a settled grief. Furthermore, they were forced to realize that they were helpless to make things better: and such a realization gives to the observer of an unhappy marriage a pang which, bad as their condition may be, the principals do not know.

The summing up of it all was that Paul drank. There could at last be no doubt of this. It

was the day the baby was buried that Miss
Sarah's eyes were pitilessly opened to it. She
had gone out with him to the cemetery, and had
come back touched in spite of her resentment.
He wept, she told her sisters afterwards, as he
carried the little coffin in his arms from the
carriage to the grave; and when they came home
to Annie, and to the house where the shadow
seemed still to linger, Paul was so absorbed in
his grief that he was entirely forgetful of her
presence, and "quite gave way," Miss Sarah
said, in that awed voice with which a woman
comments on a man's tears. "And then," she
went on, "I thought in the evening that he
seemed very much moved; he was leaning his
head on his hands, and did not answer when I
spoke to him, and I was quite alarmed, fearing
that he was in a swoon. But I went up to him,
and — his breath — I — I — realized what it
was," sighed Miss Sarah; "and such conduct
shows he did not love the dear little baby."

"Oh, poor Annie, poor child!" said the sisters.

They never dreamed, these four tender women, how Sarah's pity, her very presence, had
been an intolerable burden to Annie. That
well - meant, tender intrusion of pity which
comes to the woman whose trouble lies between
herself and her husband, too deep to be reached

by any outside comfort, rouses sometimes a helpless impatience, almost an irritation, that has to be smothered under perfunctory acceptance and vague acknowledgments of kindness.

Annie drew a long breath of relief when her sister went away; and then she cried for very pity of herself that she could not feel that old dear regret of missing Sarah. She was glad she and Paul were alone again, alone with their grief for the little baby and with the absorbing interest of living.

Very likely, Annie, in the stress and strain of her life, never quite realized how her sisters suffered because of her suffering. Little by little, as time went by and she did not see them, and their pleasant, gossiping letters came into circumstances of which they had no comprehension, and touched with chattering, tender lightness upon subtleties of human nature which they could not understand, little by little they grew unreal to her. Sometimes, with sad self-consciousness, she felt that her love for them was the child's love for the things of childhood. It was through no fault of theirs or hers; it was the inexorableness of time. Instead of living tranquilly in the old house, set in its quiet garden, with her Sunday-school class for a vital interest, her bits of fancy-work and her improving reading, her calm, amiable interest in her neighbors, Annie had been looking into the depths of a human soul.

She knew that if she could open the parlor door some evening, and join the lamp-lighted circle about the table, she should find the old life again, as it had always been. She knew the very gesture with which Miss Sarah would open the evening paper, and she could hear Nannie's invariable question, "Well, who's dead and who's married, sister?" and then the comments on the news, shrewd and sometimes a little severe, but quite devoid of any knowledge of life. She could see the satisfied air with which Miss Emily would shake out some bit of fancy-work and say, "There! I've done three fingers to-night!" and she would find herself smiling as she remembered the deep interest of the moment when Mary's market-book would be opened for accounts, and for comments, and for surprise at the butcher's charges. It would all be the same; yet what a stranger she would be if she joined the group about the table!

Her very tenderness for her old life declared that she had become its observer; and the moment that the consciousness comes, of observing Life, or Love, or a situation, the candid mind knows that it is an outsider. It was this recognition of alteration in herself which was the real pang to Annie; in finding herself she had lost her sisters, although they did not know it. She knew they thought her unhappy; she knew that by no possibility could she ever make clear to them the happiness which brooded in her heart, the exultation of her knowledge of her husband's nature, — a certainty of knowledge which even Paul could not shake.

"Why do you believe in me?" he cried out to her once. "Don't trust me, don't believe in me, Annie!"

"It is because you are you, Paul," she said patiently.

"But you don't know me!" he said, with the voice of one who tries to throw off some burden. "Why can't you let me go? I am not what you think I am. Let me go."

"I will never let you go."

"You'll have to, some time," he said brutally. But Annie could meet that without flinching.

Perhaps her patient insight taught her how he might chafe under the restraint of her ideal of him, and so she could make allowance for his irritation; or perhaps she called it humility, and believed in him the more for it. Love can do such things. But one falls to questioning whether such love can realize that the idealization which holds a man up to his best, despite himself, has all the danger of the stimulant.

Certainly, Love's splendid courage rarely stops for such reasoning, just as it is rarely generous enough to allow its beloved to create his own ideal.

"See what I've brought you to!" said Paul, lifting his face from her knees, and flinging out one trembling hand.

"Yes; and it's all wrong, Paul. But some day it will stop."

Her faith seemed to dazzle him; he put his head down again, and lifted the hem of her dress and kissed it. "I'll go in to the Picture," he said after a while. "Bring me my palette; I'll go to work."

Her face lightened as a flower beaten by rain lifts itself to sudden sunshine. But he glanced at her with half-wearied, half-contemptuous pity. "What do you make of my work being best after a spree?"

Only the smile in her eyes answered him.

It was no wonder that Paul was stung when he looked at Annie's surroundings. Annie Murray had never known the forlornness of "trying to get along" until he had taken her happiness and comfort into his keeping. But she learned it then.

They had boarded for a time after the baby died, and then lodged; but even Annie quailed at that kind of life, and now, at last, they had

drifted to the top floor of a building given up
to many small businesses, and little personal
industries.   It had been a private house once,
and it had still a curious reserve and dignity
about it, though the crescent of leaded glass
above the entrance was broken in one or two
places, and the slender fluted columns on either
side of the battered white door were defaced and
grimy.   The rooms on the lower floors were of
stately height, darkened about the ceilings by
heavy cornices, from which the gilding had
chipped and fallen, and where for years the dust
had heaped itself.   The staircase curved with a
beautiful sweep, and the hand-rail kept as fine
a polish as though the careful eyes of the mis-
tress, dead these fifty years, saw that the foot-
man should do his duty to the mahogany; the
ceaseless slip of hurrying hands accomplished
this, even as the stumble of rough feet had worn
the bare oak of the stairs down to the splintered
grain.   The rooms were divided and subdivided,
except on the top floor; these, being smaller,
were let to lodgers.   Paul Calkins and his wife
had three of them, and Paul's sign was on the
rise of the first step in the lower hall: — ·

P. CALKINS,

Signs.

"We've got to live," the artist had said sullenly, when he first brushed out *Artist* and wrote *Signs*. After a while the signs became profitable to a degree which warranted the lease of the loft in the L, where a skylight in the roof, running the length of the room, poured a flood of light upon the wooden signs which he carved and painted and sold to tobacconists.

"We've got to live, and I can do these once in a while when I'm not painting," he said; and when Annie answered calmly, "No, we don't have to live, Paul. Paint, and never mind living," he swore at her between his teeth, and vowed he would never touch a brush again. He had not kept his vow, yet most of his time went to the signs.

"They pay," he explained briefly to the few people who remembered him, and recalled his strange and brilliant promise of ten years before. Such visitors saw only the signs: the Punchinellos holding boxes of cigars; the Indians with bunches of tobacco leaves, — figures executed, it had to be admitted, in no slovenly way, but with the fine precision of the man who sees the bones and muscles beneath the skin. Still, they were tobacco signs, and Paul Calkins seemed to take pleasure in showing them as his highest possibility.

A curtain hung across one end of the loft,

and once a visitor, as much through carelessness as curiosity, brushed it aside, but dropped it at Calkins's oath, and his own start at what he saw behind it.

"You paint, then — still?" he said breathlessly.

But Paul, white, and without a word, took him by the shoulder and thrust him from the room. Yes, he painted there, behind the curtain; but sometimes he did not go behind it for months, and only then, perhaps, after passing days and nights in sullen sin, in shame, or indifference, or hopelessness. Then he would paint for days, absorbed, aflame! He said of himself once that, after he had gotten his body sober, he made his soul drunk. But at such times Annie lifted her head and looked at him as a woman looks at the high priest of her soul.

She made great plans of what would happen when the Picture was done. The world should see it, should be made better by it. It was a comment on the solemn meaning of the painting to her that she forgot to plan for Paul's fame in relation to his work; it was the Picture only.

And so these last two years had passed: in the mean details of poverty; in the noisy elbowing of the life about them; in the manufacture of tobacconists' signs; in sodden and debasing weakness. But here and there, shining among

the weary vulgarity of it all, came days when
Paul drew back that curtain, and when he said
his dæmon came to him.

But Annie said that then he came to himself.

III.

It was in the spring when old Miss Sarah
said she must see Annie. "I think I am sick
for her," she said simply. "Will you write
and ask her if it is convenient, sister?" the
other three inquired.

But Sarah shook her head. "No; the last
two times we asked her that, she said it was n't.
But I must see her; I must go." And she went.

The sisters packed a dozen dainty things into
the trunk for Annie. Miss Mary made a loaf
of cake that Annie had always liked. "Do you
remember how she used to tease for it? Bless
her little heart!" said Miss Mary. Nannie was
more practical; for weeks she had been crochet-
ing a white worsted "cloud," and Sarah should
take it with her. Emily brought a big bunch
of apple blossoms, and begged Miss Sarah to
carry them in her hand. "Yes, I know they 'll
be faded; but Annie won't mind. Tell her
they came from the tree by the strawberry bed.
How the child used to love to climb that tree!
I was always afraid she 'd break her neck."

The night before Miss Sarah went, Nannie came into her bedroom with an anxious face. "Sister," she said, "we 've never thought of sending Paul anything ! "

The two ladies looked at each other in dismay. Miss Sarah was standing by her bureau, tying her nightcap under her chin, and she paused with the bow between her fingers. "Oh, Nannie, that will never do ! Annie would feel it."

"I can't think of a thing," sighed Miss Nannie.

"A book? We might buy him a book. Mary could send Betsey around to the stationer's while we 're at breakfast."

But Miss Nannie was doubtful. "It does n't seem like Paul — a book."

"The only thing that does seem like him I should n't want to carry," said Miss Sarah significantly.

"Oh, sister ! " said dear Miss Nannie.

Sarah looked contrite, but firm.

"I 'll tell you what occurred to me," said the younger sister, hesitating; "unless it would not be quite delicate?" And then she opened her hand and showed two eagles. "I got them at the bank," she said. "You girls can each give me five dollars if you want to, or else I 'll give it all to him myself. You just put it to him in a way that won't offend him. Tell him it is so hard to choose for a gentleman; and so — we ventured — we hoped he would accept — and purchase something for himself. Ask him to consider it our gift," she ended.

In the morning, what with the excitement of a journey and the pleasant jingle in their minds of their list of gifts, the sisters felt a glow of happiness about Annie; they had decided that Sarah was to induce her to come back with her and make a visit of a week. "And tell Paul we hope he can come, too," said Miss Nannie; and the others added, "Oh, of course."

And so Miss Sarah started. A sweet, timid old lady, with gray hair coming down softly upon her cheeks, and then looped back behind her ears; her black wool dress was gathered around the waist, and fell in modest fullness about her gaitered feet; she wore a shawl, and drawn on an elastic cord around the crown of her bonnet, was an old-fashioned chantilly lace veil, which fell in soft wings on either side her face. She held the bunch of apple blossoms in her lap, careful not to touch the stems any more than she could help, both to keep them fresh and to avoid staining her second best black kid gloves, which were quite loose and wrinkled, but still flat in the finger-tips, as though they had never been entirely pulled on, and so very shiny that they might almost have been mistaken for her best pair.

She was full of interest in her journey and in the people about her. She spoke to a number of women, and was sweetly unaware of their look of surprise, which, to be sure, always melted into gratification. She took a fretting child into the seat beside her, and gave him a spray of Annie's apple blossoms, and then felt in her pocket for some caraway-seed candy. The joy of seeing Annie so soon, blurred the old clear anxiety about Annie's happiness; she pictured to herself a dozen times her sister's delight at the surprise of the visit. "Bless her heart!" said Miss Sarah to herself, "how glad the child will be to see me!" She knew Annie lived in rooms: she had been told that it was the fashion now among genteel persons to live in rooms, instead of having houses to themselves, and she thought it must be quite convenient for Annie to have her kitchen and parlor and dining-room on the same floor, but she could not feel that it was altogether pleasant to have one's bedroom on a level with the kitchen. She said this to one of the ladies with whom she had made acquaintance, but the lady seemed more surprised at the locality of Annie's rooms than their arrangements. "Why," she said, "I did n't know there were any apartments down there; I thought all those old houses had been given up to business." But Miss Sarah was not concerned at that.

"It is quite unpleasant the way business creeps around old residences; we have felt it very much in Mercer. If we did not love our old house so much, my sisters and I would be crowded out, I suppose. But we are very much attached to it. My sister Annie was born there."

It was late in the afternoon when she left the train, and came out into a crowd of cabmen and carriages and a surging tide of men and women. She held her apple blossoms and her reticule in a tremulous grip, and was pallid and dazed by the rush of life about her. When at last she found herself in the shelter of a carriage, she leaned back against the cushions, and tried not to see the whirl outside. She had a weak moment of wishing that she had told Annie she was coming, so that Paul could have met her at the station. The cab jolted over cobble-stones or rumbled across brief strips of asphalt, on and on and on, until Miss Sarah wondered, in sudden fright, whether she had left the train too soon. "It would have been much quicker to have come all this distance by rail," she said to herself; and still the carriage rattled along.

The streets grew narrower, the buildings less imposing, with hints of having once been used as dwellings. Here and there, marked sharply with cheerful white lines between its bricks, a red façade, keeping still its pillared doorway

and leaded sidelights, showed itself unbroken by
the plate glass windows of a shop. It was in
front of such a house that the cab at last drew
up. The door stood open and disclosed the bare
hall: the brass bell-knob was out of order, and,
dangling from a rusty wire, hung like a once
hospitable hand broken at the wrist. The iron
hand-rail, which curved into a wrought scroll,
and then lifted into a springing arch, was eaten
with rust, and broken here and there, and the
steps themselves were flaked and worn. The
street was quite still; a belated shopkeeper on
the opposite side was drawing down a corru-
gated iron shutter over a window full of musical
instruments: a Chinaman came out of his laun-
dry in the basement of this house — which bore
the number Annie had said was hers — and
stood, his hands hidden in his flowing purple
sleeves, staring at the lady in the cab with indifferent Oriental eyes.

Miss Sarah looked blankly about; there must
be some mistake. There were second-hand
clothes in the window beside the front door, and
there was a swaying string of bird-cages hanging from a second-story sill, which bore the
sign "Wire Works." Annie couldn't live
here! It must be the wrong street. In a panic
she summoned courage to speak to a "strange
man." With a little cough, she asked a boy,

who lounged smoking in the doorway, staring
vacantly at a dusty case of tintypes fastened on
the wall, if this was the street and number to
which she had directed the cabman? The boy,
with slow indifference, "guessed it was." And
Miss Sarah, tremulously polite, begged to know
if Mr. Calkins lived here. " How do I know?"
the boy said dully. " Why don't you look at
the steps?"

"Steps?" said Miss Sarah. He jerked his
thumb over his shoulder to show her the signs
on the rise of each step, and she saw that " P.
Calkins " was on the fifth floor. Other notices
invited her, — a clairvoyant on the fourth floor,
hats re-pressed on the second, — entreaties from
all the strugglers for existence hived beneath
this ancient roof.

Sarah Murray's heart sank. She had never,
in all the sweet quiet of living, come near
enough to Life to feel its aching throb and
pulse. The shadow of humanity began to
stretch across her peace; but it took the personal expression; it was dismay that Annie
should be here! As she climbed the bare, ill-
kept stairs, that curved with a stately sweep
up to the top of the house, she stopped once and
wiped her eyes, and then resolutely stuffed her
handkerchief into her reticule; Annie must not
see any tears!

Each floor had been divided and altered to hold as many tenants as possible, and the hall windows were shut into small rooms, so that the passages were nearly dark. Miss Sarah's heart seemed to beat up in her throat; it came into her mind that she might meet a drunken person here, but she never thought of turning back. If Annie lived here, Annie's sister must know it; but her knees shook under her. She was so exhausted when she reached the top of the building that she had to stop and lean against the wall to get her breath. There was a ground-glass door beside her; she could hear people talking in the room within.

"Oh, damn you!" said a man's voice, "can't you be quiet? Your everlasting fuss is enough to drive a man to hell. I shall go out, and I shall do what I please with the money; if I double it, you can take it or leave it. I don't care."

"Oh, Paul, Paul!"

IV.

How long Miss Sarah waited, hiding in those dark passages until Paul should go out, she did not know; despair filled up the moments. Afterwards, when Annie had made her as comfortable as she could for the night, she covered her

face with her hands, and sat silently in the
dark; she dared not sob, and to the old there
may not come the easy relief of tears. Paul
would be out late, Annie said, and she would
not let her sister sit up to see him. Miss
Sarah mutely did as she was bid. Yes, they
would talk the next day, she said; Annie would
listen in the morning to all the home news; of
course that was better than talking to-night,
when the older sister was tired. Yes, yes, she
would go to bed and rest. She was afraid to
make a sound, lest Annie might hear her, for
she was in a little room, scarcely more than a
closet, opening from one which seemed to be
kitchen and dining-room and parlor in one.
She had had only a glimpse of her surroundings
by the light of the lamp Annie held, but they
told the story.

She did not sleep at all that night; all about
her beat the roar of a great city, but the clamor
in her own heart shut that out. She sat in
tense listening. After midnight the sound
came; the shuffling step, the stumbling voice.
Then the old sister wrung her hands in the
darkness.

Paul was "ill," Annie said, in the morning,
and so Miss Sarah did not see him until late in
the afternoon. He was very polite to her then,
and very tender to Annie, but he said little,

only in a low voice, once or twice, to his wife,
looking at her with those poor hunted eyes
set in a beast's face. "Annie, I must paint
to-morrow, — I *must;* you won't let any one
bother me?"

Annie's face lit and flushed. "I want sister
to see what you are doing, Paul; may I take
her in some time to-morrow?"

"Any time you wish," he said humbly.
"Anything good in my work, Miss Murray, is
Annie's; it is Annie herself!"

And Miss Murray said to herself, "He is a
hypocrite as well as an unkind person;" and
her face grew as cold as a very gentle face can.
She had brought out her gifts that morning,
except Nannie's. She could not give Paul those
two gold eagles. What! give Nannie's hardly
spared money to this drunken, cruel man, this
man who made Annie cry? No! "At least,
not yet," said Miss Sarah, despairingly aware
that she would soon have a change of heart;
Miss Sarah being one of those women who cannot long be angry, and who count such inability
the misfortune and the weakness which it is.

When Paul went into the loft to paint the
next morning, Annie talked a little about him
and about his work. Whether she knew that
Miss Sarah had discerned the signs of dissipation and was silent concerning them, or whether

she really thought her sister ignorant of them, Miss Sarah could not tell; there was no under-tone of misery in her voice, no self-consciousness of mortification. Annie said frankly that they were very poor; she had not liked to trouble the sisters by telling them about it, and she trusted Miss Sarah not to let them feel uncom-fortable or to feel uncomfortable herself; "for I am a happy woman, sister," she said.

She had been washing the dishes as she talked, and she shook the tea towel out of its damp wrinkles and hung it upon the door of the small stove. The room was very bare: there was no carpet or mat, and no display upon the walls of shining copper, such as beautified Miss Mary's domain at home. Only a well-scrubbed floor, and a sill where there was a row of bright red flower-pots, and a spotless window with a little cross-barred muslin curtain flapping across it and shutting out no pleasanter view than end-less flat roofs and great chimney-stacks and iron-shuttered windows.

"We are fortunate to get these two little rooms up here, with that tiny place you slept in. That was Paul's studio at first, and then when he began this — this other work, we took the loft at the back of the building; it is lighted from the top."

Annie stood in a stream of sunshine beside

her flowers; she had been watering them, picking off one or two dead leaves with a touch that
was a caress. "The leaves get so dusty," she
explained; "even up here, so high above the
street."

She hardly knew what she was saying; she
was groping about to find herself in relation to
her sister. She whose hands were worn with
work, whose eyes were heavy with many tears;
she who knew the brawl of the streets, the look
of the saloon where she went for Paul; she who
had grown sharp and shrewd, who bickered with
tobacconists on the price of an Indian or a God-
dess of Liberty, and who had come to look dully,
almost without pain, at the vulgarity of a cheap
and noisy business life, — what had she in common with the delicate gentility of this old sister,
who sat sewing, putting small stitches into a bit
of fine cambric, or stroking the gathers with the
careful precision of infinite leisure?

But she tried to talk; she told her sister that
Paul was engaged upon a very wonderful picture. "He has been at work upon it for two
years," she said; "but he will only touch it
when he *must*. He dare not touch it unless he
is compelled. I mean when — when he feels
just like it," she ended weakly.

"Yes, when he is in the mood," said Miss
Sarah, trying to understand.

"But of course he must earn some money; so he carves — makes figures for signs, you know — between times. It isn't his real work, of course."

"Very sensible, I'm sure," Miss Sarah replied, relieved to find something to commend.

"If he had not this reverence for his art," Annie struggled on, "he would paint pictures, just to sell them. But he won't do that. It would seem desecration to Paul."

Miss Sarah knitted her brows anxiously. "Desecration to sell his work, my dear? Why, I thought — doesn't he sell the signs?"

"Oh, they are nothing, — the signs! They have nothing to do with his art," Annie said eagerly. "He goes to his painting as a priest goes to the altar, sister; indeed, with more reverence, for I've known Paul not to touch the Picture for three months, because he was not summoned!"

Miss Sarah looked quite blank.

"I only mention this to explain the signs; you'll see them when we go in to look at the Face."

"Is the picture a face?" said Miss Sarah, thinking with a sinking of the heart of the picture above the fireplace at home.

"Yes," Annie told her; "there is more than that, but somehow I only think of the Face. I

won't tell you what it is; you must see it for
yourself."

But, as it happened, she did not see it until
two or three days later. Paul never left the
Picture, and there was nothing said of taking
Miss Sarah into the loft while he was at work,
although she, anxious to be agreeable to her
brother-in-law, proposed that she and Annie
should go and sit with him while he painted.
She went out once or twice with Annie, bravely
ignoring the dreadful flights of stairs up which
she must climb to get home, and clinging to
her sister's arm at every crossing, with a frightened clutch that told how devoid of anything
like pleasure was the sight-seeing Annie proposed. She wrote home regularly, — those
long, empty, affectionate letters which ladies like
Miss Sarah send to their families. She said
nothing of the weight that lay on her heart in
regard to Paul, — she was eating his bread, and
she must not say what she thought of him; only
that he was working "as though he was possessed," and that without any consciousness of
the truth she may have touched in the words.
She spoke of Annie's plants, and how well her
Kenilworth ivy looked; and how her wedding-
dress had been made over once, and then dyed;
and, she added, it dyed a very good black. She
told Mary that Annie used a special kind of

oatmeal, and that she had enjoyed going to market with her several times, and she observed that the market was "quite different" from the one in Mercer. She had pointed that difference out to Annie, glad to have something interesting to talk about. She talked a good deal about Mercer, and of the vicissitudes and affairs of different families; of Rev. Mr. Brown's loss of his son, of Mrs. Brown's difficulties with servants, — for Annie would remember that Mrs. Brown always had difficulties with servants. It indicated poor Mrs. Brown's breeding that she never kept her women more than a few months.

"Mamma always said that it reflected on the family to change servants," said Miss Sarah.

If Annie did not listen, Miss Sarah did not know it; it was her duty to talk, and to try to be entertaining. Perhaps Annie, weary and chafing sometimes under the soft flow of simple gossip, never realized the pathetic effort of the tender old aching heart to do her part, and "be entertaining."

Annie, in the silence of her soul, was following her husband's brush; she crept in with his food at noon, but she did not talk to him; she kept her glorying to herself; she planned again and again the scene when the revelation of Paul's nature would come to her sister. She decided to take her into the loft at noon; the light then upon that uplifted, agonized, radiant Face was best. Sarah must see it at its best. Then she would understand! Annie smiled and sighed at once. She longed that her husband's self should be recognized, and yet in the absence of such recognition she had all the exultation of the discoverer. *She* knew; she always *had* known; when the long-delayed appreciation of him should come, there would be joy and pride, but there would also be a little contempt as well.

It must have been the third or fourth day that Paul, at noon, came back across the hall, exhausted, pallid, but gentle, although remote and vague. He would not work any more that day, he told his wife, resting his hand upon her shoulder, and looking at her with contented, tired eyes. Annie silently took his hand and kissed it.

"Go out, dear; go and take a good long walk; you need it," she said; then they were silent for a moment, looking at each other as though they had forgotten Miss Sarah.

When he had gone, Annie turned eagerly to her sister; "Now you shall see it!" she cried. Her excitement brought the color into her cheeks; she looked young and happy.

When Annie opened the door of the loft, Miss Sarah was quite startled by the company in which she found herself. A half-dozen signs in

one stage of completion or another stood about
under the skylight; the sparkling day outside
fell in a long block of sunshine upon the floor,
and over it came and went gayly the shadow
from a flag on some higher building beyond.
There were pots of paint and some brushes near
the unfinished figure of an Indian, who had a
panther skin across his shoulder, and a quiver
on his back; he wore moccasins and buckskins;
there were feathers in his straight black hair,
and one sinewy hand shaded his keen eyes.
Miss Sarah did not know enough to realize the
remarkable excellence of the carving; but she
said it was lifelike. The figure of a ragged
colored boy holding out a box of cigars pleased
her more, because, she said, he was cunning;
and she liked a sailor with a bunch of tobacco
leaves in his hand. She took them all seriously.
She was truly relieved to be able to admire.
Annie waited impatiently for the examination
to end; but Miss Sarah was too interested to
be hurried. The room, low-roofed, with rafters
meeting in shadowy arches overhead, the paint-
pots, streaked and splashed with rich colors, the
strange lurking-places under the eaves for artists'
properties, were all exciting to Miss Sarah. An
old black iron lantern swung against the chim-
ney-breast, which was rough between its bricks
with ridges of plaster, on which the dust lay like

gray feathers; there was a small platform at one
side of the room, and on it was a chair of black
oak, rich with carving, and, Miss Sarah thought,
very uncomfortable; but she was too polite tc
mention that; and all about her were the tobacco
signs, standing in the oblong of sunshine, across
which came and went the shadow of the flag, or
over which a passing cloud cast a momentary
blur, like a breath upon a mirror.

A little more than half way down the room
hung the curtain, stretched from side to side.
Annie stood beside it, holding it in her eager
hand. "But, sister, this — *this* is Paul!" Her
voice trembled; she was silent a moment, as one
may bow his head before entering a holy place.
Then she drew the curtain.

She looked at Miss Sarah, but she could not
speak.

The amiable effort to be interested died out
of Sarah Murray's face; it grew gently reverent. "Why, *Annie!*" she said, and was silent
a moment; then, in a voice that dropped unconsciously, "I didn't know that Paul ever painted
religious pictures, my dear?"

"Oh, don't you understand? Can't you understand?"

Miss Sarah did not speak; then she drew a
long breath, and seemed to rouse herself. She
took off her glasses, and went quite close to the

painting, which, on the unfinished plaster of the wall, stretched all across the gable end; she touched it in one place with mild, inquiring finger. "Why, how real that is! I really thought it was sunshine. It's very strange, Annie, my dear. And — and nice, of course; though, I must say, such pictures always seem to me a little like the Catholic Church. Just a little popish, perhaps. Paul is not a Catholic, is he?" This with a faintly troubled look. Annie shook her head and turned away. There seemed to be nothing to say.

"But I'm glad he paints religious pictures, Annie," Miss Sarah said, following her. She was saying to herself that perhaps she had misjudged Paul. If he could paint a religious picture, why he must be religious, even though he did not show it.

V.

The more Miss Sarah thought of the Picture, the more perplexed she was; but she was pleased, and she made up her mind to give Paul the money Nannie had sent him; she felt she had been severe in her judgment of him. "If he paints religious topics, his conduct must be just a way he has," she explained to herself.

"Why, Annie," she said, later in the day. "I never even knew he went to church! I

thought — indeed I 'm very sorry, but I thought
he was an *infidel!*"

"He never does go to church," Annie answered, half smiling. Perhaps Sarah would
understand — in her own way. But her face
was gray and tired; it had been a great disappointment; the lonely joy of the discoverer is
not, perhaps, quite enough for the human heart.

Miss Sarah made haste to get Nannie's two
gold eagles out of her trunk, and brought them
to show to Annie, a little self-reproach tremulous in her eager, tender old voice. "I ought
to have given them to Paul before. Nannie
wants him to spend them in any way he wishes,
and call whatever he purchases a gift from her."

Annie opened her lips, and then closed them;
then she said: "Dear sister, how kind you all
are to us! Paul will be so pleased at the
thought." She glanced at the money with a
half-frightened, apprehensive look, but she gave
no hint that she did not want Paul to have it,
because of her fear that he might spend it ill;
to protect him by such a confession would have
been an insolence to the real Paul.

Miss Sarah saw the change in her face. She
did not understand it, but the old resentment at
Annie's husband came easily back. The Picture? "Well, after all, it 's better to live your
religion than paint it," Miss Sarah reflected

grudgingly, and she decided that, for her part, she believed that when artists and writers and persons of that sort put their religion into their work, there was apt to be very little of it left for their lives.

The two women sat down in the room which was used as a sitting-room as well as a kitchen, and a little silence fell between them. Annie could not put aside the fact that money coming in this way, outside his earnings, — an extra, so to speak, — would be a temptation to Paul. He would argue that if he spent it for his own diversion — Annie knew what that meant — they would be no worse but possibly better off than they were before. Annie smiled at the childishness of the excuse; traits like these had developed in her maternal love to add to that of the wife for the husband. And yet she would not treat him like a child, and offer to the man the indignity of protection. She faced all the possibilities, and, with wonderful, trembling courage, said to herself that she would not, by any artifice or excuse, hold the money back.

When Paul came home, he was still vague and abstracted. He had little to say; but the silence of a bad-tempered man is sometimes felt to be tenderness by those poor souls that love him. Miss Sarah said to herself that Paul was "pleasant," and she tried to encourage his mood by telling him that Annie had taken her into his work-room, and showed her — Paul began to frown — "the Picture. And I think it is a very nice picture, Paul. I never saw it painted in just that way. It gave me quite a different idea of " —

"You are very good," he said abruptly. "But please don't speak of it."

Annie touched the hand he had clinched upon the table, — a touch that said, "Be patient; she does not understand."

How could she? How should her simple old heart guess that comment upon the painting was like a touch upon an open eye? that his Picture was to this poor convict soul a vision of right-eousness, while he stood at judgment? He could not bear her chatter. He listened to her praise blackly, opening and shutting his hand, and gnawing at his heavy red lip. Once or twice he said, "You are very good, I 'm sure." When she had said all she could, but reserved, with a twinge of conscience, her fear that the picture was popish, she ended by saying that Nannie had sent him a little gift, and then produced the two gold coins.

Paul took them, half smiling, and lifting his black eyebrows. "I 'm afraid I 've been a bear," he said. "Miss Nannie 's very kind. Annie, write to your sister, and tell her she 's very kind. Do you hear?"

"I hope you will get something you like, Paul, and consider it Nannie's gift," Miss Sarah said.

He clinked the money in his hand, and laughed. "Annie, we might open a bank account with this. I 'll tell you! You shall have a new dress, and another pot of posies for your shelf. Will you like that? I will go and buy them to-morrow. I have a fancy that a gray dress, a silvery gray, with a sheen like water on it, would be nice? What do you say?"

Miss Sarah was lost in admiration. She saw herself writing home of Paul's generosity. Annie protested that it would be pretty, but not useful. Paul laughed, and tossed the eagles, glittering, into the air, and caught them, and stopped to examine the dates with a singular intensity, and a satisfaction that made Miss Sarah say that that was one nice thing about gold, no matter how old a coin was, it always seemed bright and clean. Annie looked at Paul in silence. If only it would occur to him to give her the money to keep! He began to talk gayly, and with animation growing in his face. He said Annie ought to dress better than she did, and that living in this poor way was a disgrace. "A disgrace to me," he said. "I ought to be doing better."

"We are doing very well, Paul." She tried

to quiet him.   "You have three orders ahead.
We must not try to get rich too fast," she ended,
trying to make her words light, and deeply,
pitifully significant, at once.

He laughed at the supper, and said that her-
ring and water-cress and toast and tea were not
enough to support life.

Miss Sarah had never seen him in such an
agreeable mood; she felt that her praise had
brought this cheerfulness, and she tried to encourage it, and also to encourage his desire for
something better.   "Dissatisfaction is very
proper when a man's poverty is his own fault,"
Miss Sarah thought, and she said aloud that she
thought a gray dress for Annie would be very
nice, although perhaps a good black silk would
be more serviceable.   "It makes over so well,"
said Miss Sarah.

"She shall have both," Paul answered,
promptly.

But his sister-in-law was disturbed at that,
for she felt sure that the quality of neither
would be very good.   Still, as Emily would
have said, it showed a good spirit in Paul to
desire to spend his own present on his wife, —
a spirit that matched the Picture, Miss Sarah
thought, much pleased.

She had never seen him in so good a light,
and she blamed herself for having been blind to

his merits before. "Not but what he has some faults which we deplore," she wrote to her sisters; "but I feel we have been too severe in our thought of Paul." She told them about the Picture; at least she said that she was pleased that Paul should have turned his mind to serious things. Then she spoke of his good intentions about the money, and gave them quite an account of the amiable way in which he had once told her how fond Annie was of her flowers, and how foolish; and how he liked to bring her a growing plant once in a while, just because she was such a goose about them.

"Did you ever see Annie wash the geranium leaves?" he had said. "She takes each leaf in her hand, and holds it, and washes it softly, with a sponge, just as if it were a baby's little palm. I believe she imagines they are children, these vegetables, just as girls play that their dolls are babies. She would n't have done it if that young one of ours had lived!" He had said this on the day which was the anniversary of the baby's death. It had seemed to Miss Sarah one of those careless cruelties of coincidence, and she had looked with quick apprehension at Annie; but Annie's face showed nothing but tenderness for a pain that was trying to hide itself beneath such pitiful flippancy.

VI.

The next few days were happy ones to Miss
Sarah. Paul was "truly agreeable," she said
to herself, with that apprehensive appreciation
which is felt by persons whose misfortune it is
to live with an ill-tempered man or woman.
He was hard at work upon his signs again, which
pleased Miss Sarah greatly. "An industrious
person is not apt to get into mischief," she assured herself. His work upon his picture had
seemed to her too much of the nature of a pas-
time. "It's as though I should spend my time
reading my Bible instead of looking after my
household," Miss Sarah reflected. "It's a
pious work, but it isn't an order; and to spend
much time upon it is idling, I'm afraid."

So she was glad to go into the loft and watch
him as he sat toiling at one of his wooden figures, and encourage him by any honest praise
which she could speak. Paul seemed pleased,
she thought, that she was so appreciative; he
certainly made an effort to induce her to express
her opinions. He said, with perfect gravity,
that he "enjoyed her conversation," and she
blushed at the compliment like a girl.

Miss Sarah was troubled that Annie showed
so little interest in the signs and in what Paul
said about them, and that made her all the more

anxious to encourage him.   So each day while
he was at work she went into the loft, and
though she glanced sometimes at the curtain
across the farther gable, she confined her attention to the figures, regarding them with that
timid respect which modest and ignorant persons
have for anything which they conceive to be art.
She was quite blind to the bad amusement in
Paul's face, or to the way in which he glanced
sidewise at Annie for appreciation of the humor
of the situation.   He was almost hilarious in
his open ridicule, which the tender old heart
never suspected.

On one especial morning he told her that he
had planned a figure of America, which was to
hold the flag of the Union, as well as a box of
cigars; but he said that he was not sure how the
flag ought to hang over the arm of the figure,
and he wondered whether Miss Sarah would be
willing to hold it for him a moment.   Miss
Sarah flushed with the pleasure of being of use.
She stood, very erect and proud, while he draped
the flag across her arm, and let its folds fall upon
her straight black gown.   She bent her mild
face down to look at it, so that the tabs of her
lace cap touched her faded cheeks; her eyes
dimmed a little, but she smiled.   She said that
she knew what the flag meant better than Annie and Paul did; they probably could not remember much of the war.

"I feel very patriotic to be a flag-bearer," said Miss Sarah, smiling at her little joke, and sure of Paul's sympathy.

Annie cried out sharply, when she saw her sister standing there among the images, her dear old face beaming with gratification in being useful, and with honor for the symbol across her arm. "Oh, Paul, *don't!*" she said. The glitter of cruel amusement in his eyes and Sarah's sweet unconsciousness hurt her like a stab. "I wish you wouldn't, Paul," she said faintly; and then she went down the room, leaving her husband and sister under the skylight, among the tobacco signs, and touched the end of the curtain, holding it in a quick, trembling grasp, as one afraid, in the darkness, seizes the hand of a friend. She never felt the need of that assurance quite as she did when she saw Paul cruel to Sarah. To have been cruel to herself was nothing; a man's unkindness to his wife may be only a lack of thought of himself. When she went back to the artist and his model, her face was pale, and she breathed as one who has struggled, but there was courage in her eyes.

"You mustn't do this to Sarah, Paul," she said; and in spite of her sister's protest, she took the flag away. "You are tired, dear sister; it's very tiring to pose. Come; let us go back to our work."

But Paul said quickly: "There! Annie! Don't move; you've put your hand just as I want it for that America. Hold it so a minute, will you? Miss Sarah, hand me that charcoal and drawing-board. There! behind you! Oh, damn! not that. Have you no eyes? There, Annie; keep it just that way."

Miss Sarah, flustered and appalled, stood beside her sister, uncertain what to do or say. Annie smiled. "When Paul wants to draw, sister, he forgets his manners. He'll be through in a minute, and then we'll go back to our work."

Paul was not disturbed by the explanation. He drew rapidly for a minute, in bold, vigorous strokes, and then he stopped, holding his charcoal poised and frowning to himself, and rose, and adjusted Annie's fingers. As he did it his face changed, and the intent look faded. "Oh, Annie! your little fingers," he said; he put his own hand upon his lips, because they quivered like a woman's, and then he took hers and laid it against his breast, fondling it, and saying: "Oh, Annie, Annie, your hand stabs me; it stabs me! How worn it is! how thin it is! Annie, it stabs me!" And then he kissed it passionately.

The love and pity in her face seemed to reach out to the poor soul struggling to escape from

the prison of his temperament, seemed to touch
and grasp him like two strong, welcoming, com-
pelling hands. It was as though Patience and
Certainty comforted him.

As for Miss Sarah, she had not waited to
hear Annie's answer. She held her head very
straight, though she felt her knees tremble as
she walked away. Paul had sworn at her! A
fine indignation lighted her old face. "That
—*person*, to use such words in our presence!"
she thought. She went back to the other room,
and took up her bit of sewing; but her needle
glanced and slipped, her fingers were so unsteady.

Paul had the grace to apologize when he came
to tea, and Miss Sarah, immediately, and with
dismay, perceived her anger melting into forgiveness. But that night she lay awake a long
time, trying to understand him. How rude and
cruel he was; how bad his temper; how dissi-
pated and profane he seemed to be. But over
and over the Picture contradicted these things
in her mind, — "a *religious* picture," she said
to herself.

Miss Sarah might not guess all that Paul had
painted into that Face upon the wall, might not
feel that his soul was there, his sin, his shame,
his everlasting hope, all that makes religion to
the man; but the subject told her that it was a

religious picture. In her own way, using simple words, with deep and dear old-fashioned terms, such as, "Has he ever had a change of heart?" "Has he really come to his Saviour?" she questioned the mysteries of a human soul.

She could not sleep, but lay listening for his step with an ache of apprehension. But when he came in, about midnight, he walked steadily, and she heard him say to Annie: "The luck's come; it's come! It will be all right now; everything will be all right. Don't worry, Annie." And Miss Sarah's fear relaxed into tired sleep.

The next day he showed a new side of his character to his sister-in-law, — a light, sweet-tempered gayety, full of small passionate tendernesses to Annie and simple kindliness to Miss Sarah herself. Annie was silent, almost to moodiness; she did not seem interested in his continued assertions that he meant to bring her a present. Miss Sarah could not understand her. She made brave efforts to rouse her sister to her duty by herself showing sympathy in all Paul said, and by one or two mild, reproachful glances at Annie.

"You bought Annie's present," she said, when he came home to supper. "That's very kind in you. You'll be so pleased, won't you, Annie, my dear?"

"You shall see it after tea," he promised her. "Annie, try and eat. Do eat this; I got it for you."

But Annie shook her head, and Miss Sarah felt really quite displeased with her.

After supper Paul brought out a package and opened it. "Annie, do look; please look," he said. "I chose it for you. I thought you'd look so pretty in it."

He shook out the gray folds, cool as moonlight upon dark ice, and shimmering in the lamplight with soft and beautiful sheen.

"I bought it out of the two eagles," he said significantly. "I assure you I did. I mean I used just that amount, and I have more left. Miss Sarah, Miss Nannie's present has grown like the five talents. I — I invested it, and more than doubled it; a good deal more! Now I'm going to give almost all of it to you, and get you to go out and buy some things for Annie. She won't do it herself."

Miss Sarah's quick delight could scarcely find words. "I've always said gentlemen understood managing money so much better than ladies. Just fancy, dear Annie, — doubled it! Annie, my dear, you should not be so dull when your husband has been successful. Pray tell me how you did it, Paul. I almost think I should like to do something of the kind with our money; except, of course, situated as we are, we can have only the safest and most conservative investments. And our money is all in trust, too, as you know."

Annie had gone into her bedroom for something, and did not hear Paul's explanation that he had doubled his money on a principle often used by churches. He would tell her about it some time, he said; and the laughter kindled again in his eyes, but died when Annie came back. Then he lifted the silk and held the soft gray folds up in this light and that, and called on them for admiration, which Miss Sarah gave unstintingly, glad to put aside for a moment a misgiving that those words about "doubling" his money began, as she thought them over, to arouse.

Paul laid the silk across Annie's shoulder, arranging it so that it fell straight and gleaming to the floor. She stood sidewise, her dark head drooping on her breast ; the long shining line of the silk, from the nape of her neck to her finger-tips and back to her heel, was full of stately grace. Her husband looked at her keenly, with the pleasure of the artist in what is beautiful; not the more human pleasure of appreciative affection. Perhaps that was why he saw the war between the soft shimmer of the gray silk and Annie's worn complexion, and said: "Annie, where's your color? You're too old for gray!"

The little period of prosperity lasted nearly a week. Paul did not work upon the signs, and no mention was ever made of the Picture. He went out early in the morning, and came back at supper-time; he was sober, but with a curious gayety about him, and the wandering, smiling eye which belongs to the man who drinks not quite enough to lose his head. Sometimes he offered Annie money, which she with sad patience refused. Once she said, "You know I won't have any part in it, Paul."

Miss Sarah wondered a little at Paul's forbearance, for she had waited a quivering instant for an outburst, and none had come. He had not met Annie's eye when she answered him; the strange vulgarity of his temper seemed cowed. He had the look of cringing away from a lash that never fell. Yet all the while he was elate and triumphant, as though a secret which he would not share filled him with self-congratulation. Miss Sarah, puzzling over the change in Annie, suddenly remembered, with a start of dismay, that speech about "doubling the money;" could it be that Paul — *gambled?*

At first this solution of the puzzle was too terrible to contemplate, but little by little she had to meet it and accept it. Then her one

thought was to get away. How could she eat
his bread? How could she sleep under his roof?
For a little while she had the strange experience
of thinking of Annie, not as her child and sister, but as Paul's wife, and feeling a certain
repulsion for them both. But this, of course,
did not last. She could have nothing but tenderness for her child; only — she must go home!
She would go on Saturday, she said, though that
was a week earlier than she had planned to
return to Mercer. Her dismay was so absorbing that she did not notice that Annie made no
effort to induce her to remain.

But Miss Sarah had to admit that, as she drew
away from him, Paul grew more agreeable. He
was very gentle to Annie, gentler than at any
time during this unhappy visit. He bought
her a bottle of wine because she looked so pale,
and half promised that he would take her to
Mercer for August.

"Traveling costs, but money's no object,"
he said. "We can afford it better now than
at any time since we've been married, thanks
to Miss Nannie."

But by Wednesday this mood had passed.
He was distrait, and plainly full of anxiety.
"It's got to turn," he told Annie; "it's got
to. You'll have to give me what money you
have. If you don't, I'll borrow it from your

sister. Don't talk! don't talk! It's done;
what's the use of talking?" They were in the
loft, and Annie gave an apprehensive glance at
the door, lest Miss Sarah, with her persistent
sympathy, should chance to enter. "A man
will come for the signs," Paul went on. "Yes,
I lost them; I lost them. Don't look at me
that way! I'll get them again. Have you
any money?"

"Only this, Paul; and I must keep it. Oh,
don't take it! Oh, how can I bear it? Paul,
I don't see how I can bear it!"

He took the money roughly, and then came
back to her where she stood, her hands over her
face, beside the figure of the sailor. There was
no sound for a moment but her broken breath
and the pattering of the rain on the long skylight in the roof; the afternoon had darkened,
and in the half-light of the dusky room the
wooden figures seemed to smile at each other
with their painted eyes.

"I can't help it, Annie," he said miserably;
"I can't help it! My God, don't you see, it is
I? I can't help it. And you'll have your
quarterly allowance next week; but I'll have
this and more back by to-night. And this shall
be the last time. I tell you it shall be the last
time. Annie, we'll go away then; just let me
get enough back to pay for moving. And I

must get these signs again. I've got to take your little money so as to get the signs; don't you see? Annie! Annie! Oh, my God! why am I alive?"

VII.

"Paul is late, Annie?"

"Yes."

"Shall you keep his supper warm for him any longer, my dear?"

"No; at least, I don't know. Perhaps I'd better. What time is it?"

Annie's restlessness brought a spot of color into her cheek; her breath came quickly; a dozen times she opened the door into the entry and listened.

All the day before Paul had been away, coming home at dusk for an hour, his face feverish with anxiety; again, to-day, he started out early in the morning, and now it was after ten and he had not returned.

"But ten o'clock is really not very late — for a man, my dear," Miss Sarah assured her sister. She could not understand Annie's anxiety, which was painfully evident; and not understanding it, she felt rebuffed and shut out. But she was too pitiful to be hurt, and too ignorantly trustful to realize how entirely a stranger to her was this harassed and haggard

woman who, with eyes full of the terrible indifference of pain, was mechanically answering
all her little questions and comments. But
Annie realized it. The effort of these past
few weeks to be all that was sweet and dutiful
to the sister who had taken her mother's place,
had suddenly betrayed itself to her as an effort.
She looked at Sarah once or twice, wondering
dully whether her sister saw how easily the
form of affection, the habit of the old life,
slipped off when a reality claimed her. She
had that terrible experience of gazing at the
familiar face opposite her, and realizing that,
despite endearing terms, despite a sacred past,
she and it were strangers.

She wished passionately to be alone. While
Miss Sarah sat sewing by the lamp, comment-
ing now and then on this or that bit of news in
the evening paper, looking at her with a distressed pity, sighing, even, her dear old face
tremulous with love, Annie could not give way
to her anxiety. Once she began to pace up
and down the two rooms, but Miss Sarah's entreaties that she should sit down and rest were
harder to bear than her own restlessness. After eleven her sister's presence grew intolerable.

"You are going to travel to-morrow, sister,
so you really must go to bed now. I'll tell
Paul you wanted to sit up and say good-night,

but I would n't let you. Oh, go — *go !* Oh —
I — I did n't mean to be impatient, but you
must not sit up any longer."

Miss Sarah protested, but went. It seemed
strange to her that Annie preferred to be alone
when she could have company.

"I hope she knows I'd have gone into my
room, so as not to see him, if — if he was over-
come," she thought, a little hurt at Annie's apparent distrust of her delicacy. She went to bed,
but she could not sleep; she lay there with an ache
of pity in her heart that trembled into prayer.
She said to herself those words that some time
or other falter on every human lip, — "The
Lord's providences are very mysterious!" and
then the questioning wonder: Why had He
not taken Paul, instead of that precious baby?
How happy they would have been by this time
if He had but seen fit to do what human wis-
dom so plainly approved. Annie would have
come home to live, and by and by she would
have grown resigned ; and how the sisters would
have loved the child! "And we would have
brought it up so carefully," sighed Miss Sarah. But instead, Paul had lived, — had lived
to break Annie's heart by his drinking and
his gambling and his rude temper. She said
to herself that even though it was terrible to
go and leave Annie with him, she could not

help feeling the relief of getting out of his
house. "His food chokes me!" she thought,
violently. She could hear Annie pacing up
and down, and called out to her once to go and
rest; but Annie answered that she was just
going to open the door a moment and listen;
she thought Paul must be home soon. She did
listen; she went out into the hall, and, leaning
on the balustrade, looked down the spiral of the
staircase. A window closed with a clatter on
the floor below her; the wind sighed somewhere;
down in the lower hall there was a noisy burst
of laughter and a good-natured scuffle. The
gas jet, from a thin iron arm that crooked out
of the whitewashed wall where the stairs curved,
flared in some mounting draught.

Annie, listening, leaned her head against the
wall. She wondered if in all these years the
old house had held a pain like her pain. Most
people have this thought once in their lives, at
least. The house was a hundred years old, she
had been told; time enough for Sorrow to have
gone up and down these stairs many times. She
wondered if any other woman had leaned her
head against the wall, dumb with pain. Death
had stricken human love here many times, but
what was death? She wondered how it would
seem to her if Paul died? She would feel his
freedom from the fetter of his temperament,—

feel it like a full breath ! And then she started,
with that curious misgiving that is a sort of
superstition, — the fear of her own thoughts.
She went back to look at the clock. It was
after one. A little later, Miss Sarah, dozing,
heard a noise, and started up, crying out to
know what was the matter.

"I am a little worried about Paul. I am
going out to meet him. There's nothing the
matter, but I must go and meet him."

"Go *out!*" said Miss Sarah, standing in her
doorway, a gaunt, anxious apparition, "Annie,
my child! at this time of night? Why, what
are you thinking of?"

"I'll be back soon, I'll be back soon," she
said mechanically. She was putting on her
bonnet with intent haste.

"Oh, Annie, Paul would not wish it. At
night, you — on the street! My dear, I must
go with you. I cannot allow — Paul would
never forgive — Why, Annie, it's nearly
two, my dear!"

"Sister, if he comes in, be sure not to let him
go out again."

"Annie, Annie, come back!" Miss Sarah
called, in quavering remonstrance. But Annie
had gone.

Miss Sarah could do nothing but look down
the stairs after her, and then go back to her

room. She sighed, and the tears stung in her
eyes. She was very much frightened, but not
so much so as she might have been had she not
taken literally Annie's words that she was going
to meet Paul. She thought that meant that
Annie knew just where to find him, and that
they would return together immediately. Still
she was greatly disturbed. Annie was out, at
night, alone, alarmed about her husband!
Annie, her child, whom she had guarded and
loved so tenderly that she would not have had
her know that such pain could be in life! She
wondered how she could ever tell the girls the
truth about Paul. How could she tell them of
his dissipation, of the way in which Nannie's
money had gone? Sitting here alone in the
kitchen, her resentment burned too hot for
tears. After a while she tried to read, for her
eyes were growing heavy, and she must not be
asleep in case Annie, by any chance, should
come in before Paul; but the letters ran together in a mist. "Dear me! this will never
do," said Miss Sarah; and got up, and began
to move about the room, but stopped, thinking
she heard Annie's step. There was the heavy
roll of a carriage in the street, and then the
clock struck two; but the house was silent.
Every moment she fancied she must hear them
coming upstairs together. She was a little

chilly, a little nervous here alone. The weight of grief for Annie's grief oppressed her too much even for prayer. She would let her eyes close for just a moment, she thought.

She did not know how long she had been asleep when there came a leaping step upon the stairs, a run through the entry, and then the door opened with a burst, and Paul leaned, gasping, upon the knob.

"*Annie?*"

Miss Sarah, her eyes blurred with sleep, stammered something.

Then he groaned aloud and threw up his hands. "Tell her I lost — *it*. But I stabbed him: he shall not have it! Tell her — I loved her. Tell her — *tell* her there's only this one thing I can do. Oh, she'll understand — she'll understand" — He stopped with a curious cry, and turned and ran, crouching, across the entry to the loft.

Sarah Murray stood staring at the open door, seeing her own shadow flicker on the wall, hearing down in the street a song trailing into silence, as some light-hearted reveler went on into the night.

"Paul has stabbed some one? Paul? Annie's husband has" — She did not understand; she was faint for a moment. What did it mean? "He has lost 'it.' What? He has

been gambling again ! " In the whirl of confusion she never thought of the Picture; only
one word stood out clearly. Paul had *stabbed*
some one.

Then her strength came to her, and she went
out, across to the loft door, and knocked, and
said: "Paul — I — don't understand. Paul ! "

But there was no answer, and in a panic she
fled back again, and even locked the door, in
sudden, unnamed terror. But she sat beside
it to be ready to slip the bolt for Annie. She
had not long to wait.

Miss Sarah never knew how she said what
she had to say, with what terror and loathing
she repeated Paul's words to his wife, — Annie
standing, just as Paul had stood, clinging to the
door-knob, gazing at her in wide-eyed silence.
Few words, each falling on the heart like a drop
of anguish. As she spoke, she tried with trembling old hands to lead her sister into the room,
but Annie broke away without a word. Sarah
followed her, and then stopped, and went back
and hid her face. But that was only for a moment.

The entry was dark, save for the blue flare
of the gas that made a nimbus of light around
Annie, kneeling against the loft door. When
Miss Sarah, sobbing, knelt down beside her,
Annie did not seem to see her,

"Paul, I am here. Paul! Tell me the truth."

Miss Sarah could not hear his answer, but Annie heard it.

There was silence for the space of a heart-beat, and then Annie lifted herself, crying to him hoarsely to let her come in. "Oh, Paul, *I love you* — let me come in. I love you — I love you — Paul, let me come in. I did n't doubt. Only — I — I could n't breathe for a moment. Let me in, Paul!" But there was no sound. "Paul, Paul, I love you. Only — for an instant — I could not speak. *I love you.* Let me come in!"

But he did not answer. Sarah called to him once, for God's sake, to speak to Annie; but there was silence.

How still the city seemed in that breathless hour before daybreak! The white cold dawn brought a sigh from the sleeping streets. A wandering sound crept now and then through the house. A door opened and closed; and then everything was still again.

Paul had spoken twice. Miss Sarah did not come near enough to hear that terrible confidence between husband and wife. After it, Annie did not cry out to be allowed to enter; she only spoke to him sometimes, gently, with ineffable tenderness, in some soft caress of

words, as a mother speaks to a child. They
heard him move away from the door once, and
then came a strange sound, as of canvas being cut or torn. And Paul's wife lifted her
face with terrible assent and understanding.

A little after dawn the men came to take him.
Annie stood up, her arm across the door, the
other hand entreating the officers to pause.

"Paul, let me in first!" she called once,
with an agonized voice. There was no answer.
Then she moved aside to let one of the officers
put his shoulder against the door, which bent
and quivered, but held, and then crashed in.

Then she touched the man on the arm.
"Wait. I must go first. There is no other
door than this. Wait." She seemed unconscious that they followed her into the room, and
then paused, huddled in a startled group in the
doorway. There was no need for them to guard
against his possible escape.

There was no sound. The dawn lay white
under the skylight, — upon the motley figures; upon a candle, still burning with a pallid
flame ; upon the long heap of the fallen curtain,
and upon the defaced and ruined Picture on the
wall. The men bared their heads, and one
looked away, and another swore, and one turned
faint. They watched her as she knelt down
and took him in her arms. "Yes, yes, I un-

derstand," she seemed to assure the still face.
And then she lifted her own, shining with a solemn elation, and looked at the place where the
Picture had been. Her justification spurned
words. His mute lips told of the warfare of
his soul against his body; the ruin on the wall
said divine things. She had no need to speak.
And cradling the poor dishonored head upon
her breast, she kissed his lips.

And then content made reverent way for
grief.

ELIZABETH.

MR. THOMAS SAYRE had a very disagreeable moment when he learned that his mother had chosen to rent to an artist the top floor of her old house in Bulfinch Court.

"You had no business to let her do such a thing, without first telling me," he said sharply to his sister. "Mother only had to speak, and I'd have given her all the money she wanted."

"But mother never would speak, you know, Tom," Elizabeth Sayre answered gently; "and it scarcely seemed necessary, either, for you knew exactly how much her income was lessened when the bank failed."

"Well, suppose I did? I didn't think — I mean, I didn't realize" — He paused. His sister did not reply, but her silence was significant. "You ought to have reminded me," he ended sullenly.

And indeed there was some excuse for his annoyance. He had come home on his first visit, after an absence of several years abroad,

bringing with him his pretty daughter Fanny,
and anxious to give his mother some of the over-
flowing satisfaction of his own life; and, as he
told his wife afterward, "this lodger, this artist
fellow, met me in the hall, and was going to
do the honors of the house! A lodger showing
me into my own home, if you please! Mother
had not had my dispatch, and so was not looking for me."

He had scarcely waited for his mother's kiss
before he asked the meaning of the stranger's
presence; and then he stored up the vials of his
wrath, to pour them upon his sister's head,
when, later in the evening, they should be alone.

"Well," he said, after an uncomfortable
pause, "it 's lucky I 'm here now and can put
a stop to it. How long has it been going on?"

"Mr. Hamilton has been here four years" —

"He would n't be here four minutes," Mr.
Sayre interposed viciously, "if I could have
my way. But I suppose I can't turn him out
without some notice. Well, I 'll arrange it.
I 'll see him the first thing in the morning.
Oh, I 'll be civil to him, Lizzie; you need n't
be worried. Really, I don't blame the man; I
blame *you*. My mother's house turned into a
lodging-house — it 's outrageous to think that
neither you nor aunt Susan wrote me about it!"

He glanced around the room with indignant

pride. The suggestion of a lodger did seem out of place. And yet, could Mr. Sayre have known it, the greater number of the houses on Bulfinch Court had gradually fallen to such cheap ends. They kept their dignity, however, in spite of their changed fortunes; and they had that air of accommodating themselves to circumstances with calm indifference, which is as characteristic of houses with a past as it is of people. Possibly these old residences not only endured, but were even a trifle amused at the changing human life which came and went through their wide halls, and below the carved white lintels of the front doors.

Admiral Bent's house, just opposite the Sayres', sheltered dapper young clerks now in its hall bedrooms; there were dressmakers on the ground floor, and some teachers two flights up. In the admiral's time, the manners and people were different, but possibly not so interesting. A little further down on that side of the Court was a house once made reverend by the name of "parsonage." When the clergyman died, his heirs let it to a pretty widow with two flaxen-haired children and a dog; and now the two or three old families left in the Court looked at the house doubtfully, and said they wished they knew something about the inmates; but none of them took the trouble to learn anything about them by calling. The heirs, however, found that in spite of rumors, the rent was paid promptly, so they had no reason to complain. The whole neighborhood had run down. Mr. Thomas Sayre pointed that out to his father a dozen years ago, but old Mr. Sayre shook his white head.

"Your mother does n't find fault," he said.

Nor did she. Her husband found his happiness here; he loved every brick in the house, every tree on the sidewalk; the whole Court was full of small landmarks of association with his past; so, as he said, his wife found no fault, — for his happiness was hers; the quiet of the forsaken old Court was a trial to her cheerful heart, and she did resent the behavior of the children who came up out of the alley to play in the plot of grass in the middle of the square; they dropped orange skins about, and stared rudely at the occasional passer-by, or followed in solemn and ecstatic procession the ubiquitous organ-grinder in his daily tour up one side of the Court and down the other. But William loved it all, and so, she said to herself, "it was of no consequence." Afterward, when William had been taken away from her, all these small annoyances grew to have a certain beauty of their own; a deep and tender sacredness, about which she spoke to her daugh-

ter, and her husband's sister, Susan, with the
simplicity of a child: — a characteristic which
neither of her listeners shared, and scarcely understood.

Her son understood her better; yet even he
did not see that, with all the frankness of a
sweet old age, she would hesitate to tell him
that it had become necessary to take a lodger
at No. 16. A mother often feels that a child
should have the intuitive knowledge which belongs to a parent, and it seemed to Mrs. Sayre,
although she did not put it into words even to
herself, that Thomas, if he stopped to think,
would be aware of her needs; but of course,
being his mother, she found immediate excuse
that he did not stop to think. She had been
careful, during the four years that Mr. Hamilton had been an inmate of her house, to avoid
mentioning his name in her letters to her son;
so now, on this his first visit home, as he
walked up and down the sitting-room, scolding his sister to express his self-reproach, Mr.
Thomas Sayre had many things to learn.

"Yes, it's outrageous, Lizzie, that neither
you nor aunt Susan wrote to me about it," he
repeated crossly. "But I'll put an end to it,
now I've found it out for myself. I'll give
the fellow notice to-morrow!"

Elizabeth Sayre's face hardened. It was a

delicate face, and fine ; with sensitive lips, and
brown, calm eyes shining from under dark
brows; the straight, dark hair was parted in
the middle, over a tranquil forehead, and then
brushed smoothly down behind her ears; it
was a face in which sweetness was hidden by
determination, but the sweetness was there.

"No," she said quietly. "Mr. Hamilton
will remain here as long as he wishes. Mother
would be very sorry to have him go."

Her brother, his hands in his pockets, turned
and looked at her.

"Ah?" he said. The significance in his tone
was unmistakable. Elizabeth flushed like a
rose, but she looked at him with clear, direct
eyes.

"*I* should be sorry to have him go, too. He
is a very unhappy and lonely man, and if we
can cheer him, and make his life brighter, we
are glad to do it." .

"What is the matter with him?"

"He has lost his wife."

"Oh!" Mr. Sayre said blankly, but with a
little irritation as well. He was mistaken,
then; Lizzie was not "interested." "Well, I
can't help that," he said. "Widower or not,
you can't expect me to let my mother come
down to taking lodgers while I have plenty of
money."

"I should not have expected it."

Thomas Sayre flushed angrily. "Well, you've no right to reproach me; you should have told me about it. As for this artist fellow, I suppose his wife died here, and mother had all the annoyance of that?"

"No, she did not die here," his sister answered briefly; "it was before he came here."

"But he's been here four years!" cried Mr. Sayre. Elizabeth looked at him with a puzzled frown. "I mean, you said he was all broken up by his wife's death?"

"Well?"

"And she died four years ago!" He put his head back and laughed.

"Five years ago," she corrected him; "it was a year before he came here."

"Five years?" He chuckled and slapped his thigh. "My dear Lizzie, you are a great goose. I don't mean to imply that Mr. Hamilton did not regret his wife properly, and all that sort of thing; but a man doesn't sit in dust and ashes for five years, you know. It's absurd to pretend he does, and give him house-room as an expression of sympathy."

"You don't know Mr. Hamilton," Elizabeth said. "Dust and ashes may not be your idea of bereaved Love, Tom, but it is some people's; and perhaps if you had known his wife, even you might understand a grief lasting five years. She was a very lovely woman."

"He has been comforted, though, since he has been here, has he?" Mr. Sayre observed. " ' Even I ' can understand that."

He had begun to be good-natured, as he found himself amused, but his sister turned upon him.

"No; and he never will be comforted! He will never care for any one else. Oh, how contemptible you are, Tom, how " — The indignant tears sprang to her eyes; "Good-night," she said. "I think we won't talk any longer. Of course he stays here. He leases the rooms by the year. I 'll — I 'll go upstairs now. Oh, *Tom!* "

She left him without trusting herself to look at him. Mr. Sayre sat down, threw one leg over the arm of his chair, and whistled.

II.

No. 16 Bulfinch Court was on the corner where Diamond Alley came over from the thoroughfare beyond to connect it with the world. The house had been painted white once, but was a dingy drab now; the windows, set deep in the brick walls, had wide sills, upon which Mrs. Sayre kept her flower-pots and knitting-

basket, or where she could rest her book and
her after-dinner cup of tea, with that happy
disregard of order which tried the delicate precision of her daughter. There was a small
yard in front of the house, inclosed by a high
iron fence that looked like a row of black pikes,
rusted here and there, or gray with matted cobwebs, and spotted with little white cocoons. The
earth was hard and bare, except for a skim of
green mould and occasional thin, wiry blades of
grass; the continual shadow of a great ailan-
tus tree which stood in one corner, kept the
yard faintly damp even in the hottest weather,
and there was always the heavy scent of the
strange blossoms, or else of the fallen leaves.
Elizabeth tried to keep some pansies alive here
in the summer, but they languished for want
of sunshine.

On this still, hot August afternoon, the
young woman looked as languid as her dark
flowers. Her talk with her brother, the night
before, and her shame that she had lost her
temper, had been a pain that still showed itself
in her face. Mr. Sayre's indifference, too, to
her repentance (for in the morning, when she
asked his pardon, he only laughed, and said:
"Bless you, Lizzie, dear, that's all right. I
was a bear; the fellow shall stay, if you think
it wouldn't be the square thing to turn him

out "), — such indifference had pinched and
chilled her, as a burly north wind might shut
a flower. She knew intuitively that his change
of purpose had something to do with that hint
of Mr. Hamilton's being "comforted," which
had so wounded her the night before in its
slight to Love and Grief. Still, she felt the recoil of her own sharp words to her brother, as
one unused to firearms feels the recoil of a shot,
and her face betrayed the pain of self-reproach.

Thomas Sayre was out; he had taken his
pretty Fanny and gone to make some calls on
old friends, and now his mother was letting the
moments of waiting for his return melt into a
pleasant dream of her good son, her dear boy.
The windows were open, and the noises of the
alley came in. Elizabeth was moving about in
the dusk, laying the table for tea. It was too
hot for lights, and Mrs. Sayre had put down
her sewing and was sitting by the window, her
active old hands folded in her lap. Once or
twice she glanced at her daughter. Elizabeth's
unfailing precision made this task of setting
the table every evening a long one. Mrs.
Sayre lifted her hands at last with good-natured
impatience.

"My dear, when you have a husband and
children, you will really have to move about a
little quicker. Dear me! when I was your

age, I could have set ten tables in the time you've taken to set one!"

Elizabeth started, and blushed faintly.

"I didn't know you were in any hurry, mother dear," she said; and as she tried to make haste, one of the plates slipped through her fingers, striking another with that suspicious sound which tells of a nicked edge.

Mrs. Sayre looked away, and tapped her fingers on the window-sill.

"Oh, I am afraid I have chipped the willow plate!" Elizabeth said, with the sensitive quiver in her voice which always went to her mother's heart.

"Never mind, dearie," she reassured her; "it's no matter."

Elizabeth sighed, and even frowned a little in the darkness: her mother's indifference was a continual trial to her. "I ought not to have been so careless," she said, with faint severity in her voice; and Mrs. Sayre was silenced.

It was a relief to both of them when the third member of the household entered. Miss Susan Sayre was a tall, timid woman, older than Mrs. Sayre, and yet, as is often the case with unmarried women, indefinitely younger than her sister-in-law; she had Elizabeth's exactness, but with it a deprecatory tremor that gave all her actions the effect of uncertainty. Many a time

Mrs. Sayre would hold her own dear old hands
tight together, to keep from seizing some bit of
work on which Miss Susan was toiling with la-
borious and painstaking clumsiness. "It would
be so much easier to do it myself," she would
think, although she hoped she would have the
grace never to say so! "Fussy" she called her
sister-in-law, sometimes, when she felt she must
have the relief of speech. But she was glad
to see her now, because of the disapproval of
Elizabeth's silence.

She and 'Liz'beth did not seem to get along
together, Mrs. Sayre thought. Often enough,
upon her knees, she had asked herself "why?"
searching her simple heart to find her own
offense.

There is, perhaps, some psychical and uncom-
prehended reason why the truest confidences between mother and daughter are so difficult and
so rare. Usually, a girl can speak of the deepest things in her life with greater ease to any
one else than to her mother. Mrs. Sayre felt
her daughter's remoteness, but no one thought
she did. Such generous, tender, healthy natures rarely think themselves of enough importance to use the phrase of the day, and say that
"they are not understood." And yet it is very
often the case; the more morbid souls about
them are baffled by their very frankness and

openness, and are really unable to understand them; and, too often, unable also to appreciate them.

Elizabeth, loving her mother with a curious intensity which spent itself in the subtleties of conscientious scruples, was as unaware of Mrs. Sayre's longing for a more tender companionship as she was of her mother's ability to understand her; — for, quite without confidences from Elizabeth, and in spite of "not getting along," Mrs. Sayre could read her daughter's nature with wonderful clearness, although she could not explain it in relation to her own. It would have been well for the daughter could the mother have boldly broken down the reserve between them, and confessed just what she read, — confessed that she knew that the most vital interest in Elizabeth's life was Oliver Hamilton. She would have added to this that Lizzie did not know she was in love with Mr. Hamilton. Here, however, would have been her first mistake: Elizabeth was perfectly aware that she loved him. Mrs. Sayre made one other mistake, too; she said to herself, amused and good-natured and annoyed all together, that it was plain enough that Mr. Hamilton was in love with 'Liz'beth. "And there is no earthly reason why he should n't speak!" she reflected. But there was a reason, and an excellent reason, for Oliver Hamilton's silence: he did not know that he was in love with Elizabeth.

It was no wonder, though, that Mrs. Sayre's penetration failed her here. How could she suppose that her daughter's one aim had been to keep the young man blind to any such possibility in himself as falling in love? She never imagined that Elizabeth was holding him rigidly to his ideal of the sacredness and eternity of love, — an ideal which had sprung up out of his passionate grief when his wife died. That was five years ago. He had come then to Elizabeth, for she had been Alice's friend, that he might take that poor, empty, human comfort of talking of the past. He had told her all his grief, and his simple, hopeless conviction that his life was over; told it with that pathetic assertion of an undying sorrow with which human nature seeks to immortalize a moment.

Such loyalty seemed to Elizabeth so beautiful, that her reverence for it fed the flame of his devotion to his ideal, even as time began to stand between him and the substance of his grief. He did not know it, — he could not, with Elizabeth's worshiping belief in it, — but now, five years later, it was the memory of grief, not grief itself, which still darkened his life. It was a lonely life, save for Elizabeth's friendship: long days in his studio, dreaming over unfinished canvases, brooding upon anniversaries of which she reminded him; talking of an ideal love, in which he believed that he believed. And so, gradually, as his mind yielded to the pressure of her thought of him, and his life mirrored a loyalty which was hers, he began to be the embodiment of nobility to Elizabeth Sayre, and by and by the time had come when she said to herself, very simply, that she loved him; but she said, also, very proudly, that he would never love her. That "never" was the very heart of her love for him.

Surely, the last person in the world to appreciate such a state of mind was Elizabeth's cheerful, simple-minded, sensible mother. And so she continued to hope and plan for this marriage which she so much desired, and to try by small hints to "encourage" Oliver Hamilton. This hinting was, perhaps, the hardest thing which Elizabeth had to bear. Her silent endurance told of the smothered antagonism between mother and daughter, which each would have denied indignantly in herself, but was quite aware of in the other.

It had been a great relief to Mrs. Sayre to confide her desires and impatience to her son. She had done it that very morning; which accounted for his change of mind in the matter of the objectionable lodger, when Elizabeth went

to him with her apology for her quick words.
With instant good-nature, he had decided to
further his mother's hopes. With this purpose
in his mind, he had gone up to Mr. Hamilton's
studio that afternoon and looked at his sketches
with far more helpful and discriminating criticism than Elizabeth, with her wondering praise,
had ever given. Fanny went, too, hanging on
her father's arm, shyly watching Mr. Hamilton,
or answering his occasional reference to herself
in a half-frightened, schoolgirl fashion. She was
certainly very pretty, Mr. Hamilton thought.

"Pretty, and a dear child ! " Mrs. Sayre said,
watching her with the fondest pride, but with
a curious jealousy, too, for her daughter's sake.
Fanny was so gay and pretty, so light-hearted
and careless, she revealed Elizabeth's impossi-
bilities.

"Not that I 'd have Lizzie different," she assured her sister-in-law, as they sat in the darkening parlor, while Elizabeth went to get another willow plate from the china closet — "not
that I 'd have her different; only I would like
to see her enjoy life a little more."

"I don't think 'Liz'beth is unhappy," protested the old aunt, "only she just does n't show
her happiness in the way we used to when we
were girls."

"*Girls!*" said Mrs. Sayre. "You really

can't call Lizzie a 'girl,' Susy. Why, I was married at her age, and had three children. Dear, dear, I wish the child was settled!"

"Oh, now, Jane," remonstrated the other mildly, "I've always been happy, and there's no reason why 'Liz'beth should n't be, too, even if she does n't marry. Indeed, it's better to be as I am than to be unhappily married; and that is possible, you know, Jane."

"Not among nice people," Mrs. Sayre said, with decision; "not when people do their duty. And a poor husband's better than none. No woman's happy unless she's married. And then, to think here is poor, dear Oliver — Well, well, I suppose the Lord knows best."

"If you think so, sister, why don't you leave it in his hands?" said Susan piously. "The Lord will provide, you know."

"That's just it!" cried Mrs. Sayre. "He has provided, and she won't take his provision. And she's not as young as she was once, Susy, you can't deny that; little Fanny made me realize it. She's old enough herself to settle down, bless her heart! She's nineteen, is n't she? Here's 'Liz'beth," she interrupted herself, as her daughter entered; "she knows. How old is Fanny, 'Liz'beth, — nineteen?"

"Eighteen, mother; she is not nineteen until next month," Elizabeth corrected her.

"Nonsense!" cried her mother; "what difference does a week or two make? She's nineteen; and the first thing we know, she'll be getting married. I hope so, I'm sure. You need n't look shocked, my dear; I was eighteen when your blessed' father married me. I believe in early marriages, — anything to save a girl from being an old maid! And see here, Lizzie, I want Oliver Hamilton to see Fanny. I'm not a matchmaker, but there's no harm in Oliver's seeing Fanny."

She looked at her daughter with something as much like malice as could come into her motherly face. Elizabeth smiled.

"But no good, either, if you mean that he might care for Fanny."

"Oh, 'Liz'beth! 'Liz'beth! Where did you get your fancies?" cried the other. "Not from me, surely. Lizzie, second marriages are the Lord's means of healing broken hearts. Oliver would be a thousand times better off with another wife, instead of brooding over his loss. Bless me, if I had died when I was a young woman, I would have made your dear father promise to get another wife as soon as he possibly could. I always used to say that my last words would be, "William, marry again!""

"And you, mother," Elizabeth inquired, smiling, "you would have married again, if" —

"Not at all," Mrs. Sayre declared; "that's quite different. It is the men who should remarry, not the women. It's a great misfortune when a man remains a widower. I wish you'd remember that, Lizzie."

Elizabeth Sayre blushed with indignation, and made no reply. Mrs. Sayre sighed. She was glad that Tom was at home for a little while. Tom was like her, she thought.

"Neither of us will ever be as good as Elizabeth," she assured herself. And she seemed to find the assertion a comfort.

III.

Mr. Thomas Sayre knew the satisfaction of self-approval when he and his daughter turned their faces toward home. He had done his duty; he had made his visit, he had given himself the pleasure of adding to his mother's income, and now he could allow these dear people to drift into that pleasant background of his thoughts where he took his affection for them for granted. He congratulated himself, too, upon his kindness to his sister; he had done what he could to make Elizabeth happy; he had dropped a few hints to Mr. Hamilton, even going so far as to refer, casually, to the time when Lizzie would marry somebody, and his mother would be left alone. "Of course she 'll marry one of these days; I only hope it will be some fellow who is worthy of her!" said Mr. Sayre, feeling that he was very subtile, and that Hamilton must surely come to the point, pretty soon. Indeed, anxious to prove his friendliness, he had made the artist promise that when he came on to the academy with his picture, he would call upon him.

"Let us know when you 're in town, Hamilton," he said heartily; "we 'll be delighted to see you, and hear the latest news of Lizzie and the old people."

And Mr. Hamilton was glad to promise. He had enjoyed this visit. Thomas Sayre seemed like a breath of bracing mountain wind coming into his dreamy life; and Fanny gave him pleasure, too. Her fresh girlish laughter brightened all the old house, and her little foolish talk was as useless and as pleasant as the dancing sparkle of sunshine on deep, still water.

The night that Mr. Sayre and his daughter went away, Oliver Hamilton came in to take Elizabeth to prayer-meeting. This custom of going together every Wednesday evening to prayer-meeting was very dear to both these people; there was no time when they talked so freely of Oliver's sacred past as when they came out into the solemn starlight, the last words of the

benediction lingering in their reverent ears.
That night, as they walked toward the church,
Oliver began to speak of Alice almost immediately. "How it brightened your mother and
your aunt Susan, Elizabeth, to have your niece
here! Do you know, she made me think of
Alice, sometimes; there's a look " —

"Yes," she answered thoughtfully, "there is
a look of Alice. And yet, dear little Fanny
has not the earnestness in her face which made
Alice the strength that she was to those who
loved her. She was so strong. That is why
she lives in your life still, Oliver."

Oliver's quick appreciation of her words grat-
ified her, as only the confirmation of an ideal
can gratify one who loves. It brought a serious
joy into her eyes, which he noticed as they sat
side by side in the prayer-meeting, singing from
the same book, or standing together in prayer.

Oliver did not follow the service very closely.
That merry glimpse of life which Mr. Sayre's
visit had given to No. 16 lingered in his
thoughts. Ah, if Alice had only lived, how
different his life would have been! How truly
Elizabeth loved her, how truly she understood
her! What would he have done without Elizabeth? As this thought came into his mind, another followed it, as the shadow of a cloud chases
the sunshine from an upland pasture: What

should he do without Elizabeth? "When she marries" (Mr. Sayre's words suddenly sounded in his ears) — "when she marries, what shall I do?" — The shock of the idea was almost physical. He turned and looked at her; her face was bent a little, but he saw the pure line of her cheek under the shadow of her chip hat, which was tied beneath her chin with lavender ribbons. She wore a white crêpe shawl, embroidered above the deep, soft fringe with a running vine of silk; her hands were clasped lightly in her lap; her gray alpaca gown gleamed faintly in the light of the lamp on the wall above her. Elizabeth marry? Impossible! But suppose she should? What difference would it make to him? Would she not still be Alice's friend, — his friend? In this sudden confusion, his ideals seemed to evade him. Did he — did he love Elizabeth?

He felt his face grow white. He had spiritually the sensation of a man who wakes because he dreams that he is falling from a height. Oliver Hamilton's eyes were opening to life and light and a possibility. His grief was withdrawing, and withdrawing, and in its place were pain and confusion and doubt.

Elizabeth, listening to the preacher, her head bending like a flower on its stalk, was so calm and so remote that his reverence for her was

almost fear. When they rose to sing the last
hymn, and she missed his voice, she looked at
him inquiringly, and, with an effort, he followed
mechanically the guidance he had known so long.
He tried to sing, but at first he was not aware
of the words: —

> " Blest be the tie that binds
>   Our hearts in Christian love!
> The fellowship of kindred minds
>   Is like to that above.
>
> . . . .
>
> " From sorrow, toil, and pain,
>   And sin we shall be free ;
> And perfect love and friendship reign
>   Through all eternity ! "

Love, through all eternity!

"Do I love her?" he was asking himself,
and the very question seemed an affirmation.

"You didn't sing?" Elizabeth said, when
they were alone under the stars.

"No," he said shortly. She was startled at
his tone, and looked at him anxiously, but without a question. (This habit of hers of waiting
silently was, although she did not know it, a
most insistent and inescapable question.) " Elizabeth," he said hoarsely, "it has just come to
me — I — Listen ! What should I have done
without you all these years? Do you — do you
understand ? "

It seemed to Elizabeth Sayre as though for

one instant her heart stood still. But the pause between Oliver's words and her answer was scarcely noticeable.

"It has been a great privilege to me," she said, with a breath as though her throat contracted; "it is a great happiness to have helped you in any way. It is my love for Alice that has helped you."

"*Alice!*"

Oliver made no answer. They walked on, Elizabeth knowing that her hand trembled on his arm, and feeling still that clutch upon her throat.

IV.

"Why, Lizzie, are n't you going to stop a minute? Are n't you going to sit down?"

Elizabeth stood on the threshold of the parlor, her hand on the door-knob. Through her mother's words, she was listening to Oliver Hamilton's step as he went up to his studio. Mr. Hamilton had left her at the front door, and gone at once to his rooms, instead of stopping as usual for a chat with Mrs. Sayre. The rest of their walk home, after that word "Alice," had been full of forced and idle talk, which covered the shocked silence of their thoughts.

Mrs. Sayre's voice now seemed to her

daughter like a stone flung into a still pool,
which shattered the silence, and let loose a
clamorous repetition of this strange thing Oliver had said, or rather this terrible thing which
he had left unsaid. Elizabeth leaned against
the door, holding the knob in a nervous grip.

"Come, child, sit down and tell us about the
sermon," Mrs. Sayre commanded her, cheerily.

"No," Elizabeth said, "I only stopped to say
good-night. I — I am rather tired."

"Why, what's happened to Oliver?" said
Mrs. Sayre. "Why does n't he come in a
minute? Have you and Elizabeth quarreled,
Oliver?" she called out good-naturedly, thinking him still in the hall.

Elizabeth turned abruptly.

"Good-night," she said, and a moment later
they heard her light step on the stairs.

Her mother and aunt looked at each other.

"I believe they *have* quarreled, Susy. Why,
she did n't kiss us good-night," said Mrs. Sayre,
in rather an awed voice.

Elizabeth, in the darkness of her bedroom,
stood still in the middle of the floor, her fingers
pressed hard upon her eyes: her heart beating
so that she could hardly breathe. The white
crêpe shawl slipped from her shoulders, and fell
like a curve of foam about her feet. The light
from the street-lamp, which flared in an iron

bracket on the corner of No. 16, traveled across the worn carpet, and showed the spare, old-fashioned furnishing of the room; it struck a faint sparkle from the misty surface of the old mirror, and it gleamed along the edge of a little gilt photograph frame that was standing on the dressing-table. Elizabeth, shivering a little, the soft color deepening in her cheeks, and her eyelashes glittering with tears, saw the flickering gleam, and, with a sudden impulse, lifted the photograph, holding it close to her eyes and staring at it in the darkness. But the light from the lamp in the court was too faint to show the face. With an unsteady hand she struck a match and lit her candle. She had forgotten to take off her bonnet; she stood, the light flaring up into her face, looking with blurred eyes at Alice's picture. At last, with a long sigh, she kissed it gently and put it again on the table. Then she sat down on the edge of her bed, staring straight before her at the candle, burning steadily in the hot, still night; her hands were clasped tightly upon her knees.

It was long after that — it must have been nearly midnight — that Mrs. Sayre heard a step in her bedroom, and said, with a start: —

"What is it? Is that you, 'Liz'beth?"

"Yes, mother dear. I — I wanted to kiss you; I wanted — you!"

Mrs. Sayre gathered the slender figure down into her arms.

"Why, 'Liz'beth! Why, my precious child! Are you sick, my darling?"

"No, no," she answered, a thrill of comfort in her voice; "only I didn't kiss you good-night. I ought n't to have wakened you. Good-night, mother darling."

"But, Lizzie," said the tender old voice, "something troubles you, my precious child. Did Oliver"— She felt the instant stiffening of the arms about her, and her daughter drew herself away.

"There's nothing the matter, mother dear," she said, her breathless voice quivering into calmness. "You will go to sleep now, won't you? I ought not to have disturbed-you." And she had gone.

Mrs. Sayre sighed. "I wish I could learn not to speak about him," she thought. "Yet if she would only tell me!"

But nothing could have been more impossible. Alas for those natures that cannot give their sorrow to another! Elizabeth longed for sympathy and comfort, yet she knew not how to open her heart to receive it. Such natures suffer infinitely more than those happier souls whose pain rushes to their lips.

Elizabeth's struggle with herself had ended

when she sought her mother; she knew what she must do. She said to herself with exultation that she loved Oliver with all her soul; loved him enough to help him to be true to himself. He had told her, oh, how often, in those earlier days, that to him marriage was for eternity as well as time; that Love, from its very nature, could not be untrue, and so there could be but one love in a life. "If a second comes," he used to say, "either it is an impostor, or the first was; either the first marriage was not sacred, or the second will not be!" She remembered how she had heard him say once of a man who had suffered as he had suffered: "No, his living is over; he can remember, but he cannot live again. If he dares to try, life will be ashes in his mouth!"

Should she let him try? Should she let him think that his love for Alice was not love, or his love for her was disloyalty to Alice? How plain, how easy, was the answer, just because she loved him!

V.

The next morning Mrs. Sayre looked at Elizabeth anxiously. It was evident that her daughter suffered, and she longed to find one weak spot in that armor of reserve where she might pour in the oil and wine of love. But

Elizabeth's face had settled into the invincible calm which sympathy dare not touch. Indeed, her mother would even have wondered whether her suspicion, in that hurried kiss at midnight, had not been all wrong, had it not been for Mr. Hamilton's manner.

Oliver Hamilton was too confused and dazed by his own possibilities to take thought of what his face or manner might betray; he said to himself that Elizabeth did not know what self-knowledge had leaped into his astounded brain in those brief words of his. But he would tell her; only, not to-day, — not to-day! He did not doubt that he loved her, — at least he loved Love; but to love her, gave the lie to five years' protestations!

Elizabeth made no effort to avoid him. She believed so firmly in his loyalty to the past, — a loyalty so beautiful that it had kindled in her the very love which it denied, — she believed so entirely in him and his love for the dead Alice, that she would not permit herself to doubt that his thought of her was only a fleeting fancy.

To avoid him was to confess a fear that it was more. So when, on Sunday afternoon, he suggested that they should go out and walk across the bridge and along the road that led over the marshes, she assented with pleasure; a pleasure

in which, when they started, there was a thread
of irritation, because she knew, as they walked
down the Court, that her mother and aunt
Susan were looking after them, and speculating
as to whether Oliver was "going to speak."
She was glad to turn into the first side street,
and lose the consciousness of the eyes that were
watching the back of her head. It was that
sense of relief that made her draw a long
breath, and Oliver instantly turned and looked
at her with a solicitude in his eyes which was
new.

"Are you tired?" he said gently.

"No," she answered. She saw that the hour
she had refused to think possible was coming;
yet it should not come! "Oh, Oliver," she
said hurriedly, "I wish you would make a
study of the marshes in September; there is no
autumnal coloring so lovely as those stretches
of bronze and red, with pools here and there
that are like bits of the sky. Suppose we try
to find just what you want, this afternoon, and
then this week you can go to work. I wish you
would really and seriously begin to work."

"I want to, now, myself," he said soberly.
"I have wasted too much time. Elizabeth, I
have lived in a dream."

"Yes," she agreed, wondering whether the
unsteadiness which she felt in her voice could

be heard, "I know you have. I have been thinking about it lately, and I wanted to say to you — I know you will forgive me for Alice's sake, if it seems a hard thing — I wanted to say to you that it seems to me you ought to make your grief an inspiration in your life, not a hindrance. It ought to mean achievement, not a dream, Oliver."

He did not answer her, and when, a little later, he began to speak, it was of something else.

The walk across the marshes was toward the east; the city lay behind them, and the little tidal river, catching a faint glow on its darkening expanse, wandered on ahead, fading at last into the cold violet of the distant hills.

"Oh, this is what you ought to do," Elizabeth said, as they paused a moment, and turned to look back at the town, whose windows flared with a sudden ruddy blaze. The housetops were black against the yellow sky; a cross upon a distant spire flashed, and then faded into the sunset. The sea stretched its fingers in among the marshes, and rifts of water shone blue with the faint upper sky, or fiercely red where the clouds along the west were mirrored. The salt grass had bronzed and bleached, and had a hundred rippling tints of dull purple or warmer russet. Some of it had been cut, and lay in sodden yellow swaths, and some had been gathered into haystacks, that stood here and there like little thatched domes. A group of boys were playing down by the water, and their black figures stood out clear against the amber sky; a tongue of flame from their bonfire leaped up, red and sharp, and lapsed again; and the lazy trail of white smoke, lying low along the marsh, brought to the two watchers the faint delicious scent of burning brush and drift.

"Oh, couldn't you do this?" Elizabeth said, breathless with the joy of color. "Oh, how wonderful the sky is!"

But Oliver, instead of planning for a picture, was staring into her face.

"Elizabeth," he said, "I want to tell you — something. When I said I wanted to begin to work, did you understand what I meant? My past, you know what it is to me, but — Oh, Elizabeth" —

She turned her eyes away from his, but she answered calmly: —

"Yes, indeed I do know what it is to you, Oliver; and it is your present, too, — I know that. I know how real Alice is to you. It is she who makes your life now, just as she has made it in the past, and will make it in the future."

He opened his lips to speak, but he had no

words, only blank impatience at the impossibility of putting aside that sacred name; and yet he was aware of a curious willingness to accept the check; he could not understand himself.

"Ought we not to go home?" Elizabeth was saying gently. "See how gray the marshes are getting."

He shivered.

"Yes, come."

The walk home was very silent.

VI.

The yellow elm-leaves were thick upon the ground in Bulfinch Court, when September, weary with its noon heats, held out an entreating hand to cool October. Mrs. Sayre found it necessary to have a fire occasionally in the evening, and she could not understand why it was that Oliver Hamilton did not sometimes ask to join the little circle about the hearth.

"He used to, last autumn," she complained. "What's the matter, Lizzie, — what does it mean?"

The anxious interest in her mother's face offended Elizabeth Sayre; "Have you refused him?" it said. "Have you had any disagreement?"

The indestructible tie between mother and

daughter was sadly strained in those fading fall days. Elizabeth had withdrawn more and more into her own life; and she was too eager in her reticent living to know how cruelly she put her mother aside. The thought of Oliver Hamilton shut every other thought out. He loved her! Here was glory and sweetness, but pain and disappointment as well. His love for the dead Alice, his serene and lofty loyalty, in which Elizabeth had so rejoiced, — where were they? Yet they should not cease! He must be true to his own ideal, she said to herself again and again; he must conquer this passing unfaith.

With this determination tingeing every action and word, absorbing every thought, it was no wonder Mrs. Sayre felt shut out of her daughter's heart. Elizabeth lived, in those fall days, only to turn Oliver back to his own better life. In all her talks with him, as they went to prayer-meeting, or wandered through the picture galleries, or came home together from the library, there was this strange fencing and parrying. How many times, when she thought she saw the words trembling on his lips which would make him untrue to his best self, and bring her the sweetness of human love, had she turned his thoughts back to Alice! How many times, when the door to happiness had seemed about to open, had she closed it with that single word, "Alice"!

Alice! Alice! The name rang in her ears; it seemed to her sometimes as though she hated Alice.

This suppressed excitement told upon her; her face grew paler, and there was a weary look in her eyes which her mother noted with anxiety. Mrs. Sayre almost betrayed her satisfaction when, one evening late in September, Oliver told her that he was going to New York for a fortnight, and promised her to call upon her son, while he was there. He told Elizabeth gloomily, that he was glad to get away; life was a miserable puzzle, he said, and he was going to forget it for a while if he could.

Her face brightened. "I am so glad you are going!" she said. It was well that he should not see her for a time, she thought; he would have regained his old faith before he came back again.

The look of relief in her face did not escape him.

"She does n't love me," he said to himself. "Well, I will not urge her, I will not trouble her: but our friendliness is over; it can never be the same again."

Of course he was right. He was wakening to find himself still a man, although he had slept so long beneath his cloak of sorrow that he was yet half blind and dazed; and he knew that he and Elizabeth must be either more to each other, or less.

It would have been hard for him to say which was the stronger in his mind, his conviction that he was yet capable of love, or his shame that his love was capable of death. It was this confusion of shame and exultation and pain that made it easy for Elizabeth to check the words which came again and again to his lips. This sudden vanishing of the darkness of unreality left him groping in a blaze of light; he was full of bewilderment. He could not live as he had been living; he dared not think of Alice; — it seemed as though his love for Elizabeth had masqueraded beneath the thought of Alice!

But Elizabeth felt a burden lifted when he went away.

"It will be all right when he comes back," she said to herself; "he does not know that I saw it, and he will forget it." And so she fell into the old round of duties, and she and her mother came a little closer together, only jarring apart again when Mrs. Sayre mentioned Oliver Hamilton in any way. But by the time his two weeks' absence had lengthened into three, and the fourth was just opening, Mrs. Sayre had learned, she said to herself, to hold her tongue, and so she and her daughter came to know something like friendship, as well as the love which had always been theirs.

"But I would like to know what keeps Oliver," she confided to her sister-in-law, as they sat beside the fire, in the Saturday evening dusk. "'Liz'beth won't let anybody see that she misses him, but she does."

Susan shook her head doubtfully. "I think Lizzie's glad he's gone. I can't say why; but that's how it seems to me."

"Well, Susy," interposed the other with amiable contempt, "you can't be expected to be a judge — *you*. But I, being married, understand such things. She misses him terribly, my dear. Well, I'm glad there's a letter from him to-night. I wish she'd come home and read it to us."

Susan leaned forward and stirred the fire gently.

"I'm not married, Jane, I know," she acknowledged humbly; "but sometimes I think 'Liz'beth feels *proud* because Oliver's faithful to the deceased?"

Mrs. Sayre took off her glasses and polished them quickly on her black silk apron. Her handsome black eyes snapped.

"Susy, if you weren't *born* an old maid, you never would have thought of anything so ridicu-

lous!'" She picked up the unopened letter from
the table and looked at it longingly. "Dear
me! I wish I knew what was in it. It's thick
enough to be an offer, and"—

She did not finish the sentence, for Elizabeth
opened the sitting-room door. The faint glow
of the fire dazzled her eyes, fresh from the rainy
darkness of the streets, so that at first she did
not notice the letter. Her mother, however,
accustomed to the half-light, could see her
daughter's face, and was troubled by its pallor.

There was a reason for it; a new pain had
come to Elizabeth in her walk home. She had
gone out early in the afternoon to visit a sick
Sunday-school child; but, the call made, she had
stood hesitating in the doorway of the tenement
house. There was nothing of importance that
she must do; there was no other visit which
must be made. She might as well go home.
But she was strangely restless; she did not want
to go home. The thought of sitting by the fire,
watching the rainy evening gather into darkness, while her mother and aunt Susan talked
about Oliver, was unbearable. She had borne it
often in the past, but then Oliver had been in
the house; while they were speaking, she could
listen for his step upon the stairs, or the sound
of the studio door closing, and then the echo
jarring through the empty halls. But how dif-

ferent it all was at No. 16 Bulfinch Court without him! All her life seemed bleak and useless, filled only with that gentle chatter over cups of tea by the fireside. No, she could not go home just yet. The rain beat against the houses on the opposite side of the street, and there was a gush and gurgle from the tin spout that carried the water from the gutters under the eaves. A sudden gust of wind twisted the loose folds of her umbrella into a wet spiral; she shook it and opened it, and then found herself plodding out into the rain.

She missed Oliver with a sort of sick pain about her heart which she did not understand. "It's enough happiness to love him, even if he does n't love me," she assured herself, as she had done many times before, never doubting her own sincerity. Ever since she had recognized her love for him, she had been holding with all her might to this belief which human experience gives us the right at least to doubt, — that the human heart can be satisfied to give love, when it receives none in return.

Elizabeth, walking aimlessly into the storm, feeding the hunger of her heart with this assertion, found herself at last on the road that led over the marshes.

The sky was low and dull; the gray rain was sweeping in from the sea, and through the sod-

den grass the winding fingers of water were blackening at the touch of the wind. The memory
of the yellow August sunset came back to her,
and Oliver's words; she bit her lip, and the
landscape blurred as though with some sudden
driving mist.

It is hard enough at best to keep the exaltation of sacrifice in one's daily commonplace
living; but when into that commonplace living
creeps the suggestion that the sacrifice has been
unnecessary, then a sick bewilderment falls upon
the soul. This suggestion came now, suddenly,
to Elizabeth Sayre. Perhaps she had made a
terrible mistake? If Oliver loved her, whether
he put it into words or not, — if he *did*, was
not the untruth to his ideal come? Would any
hiding it from herself and him do away with
the fact? Merely to keep him silent could not
make him loyal to Alice.

Elizabeth caught her breath as one who sobs,
and yet with a strange, sharp pang of joy.
Oliver, by all those unuttered words, was hers!

But she would not allow herself to think such
thoughts. Her mind was in a tumult; she
doubted her own sincerity. She turned and began to walk back to town. She was very tired;
her dress was heavy with dampness, and her face
wet with rain; her tears were hot upon her
cheeks. No one noticed her in her long walk

across the marshes; the occasional pedestrian cared only to shelter himself behind his umbrella, and did not look into the faces of young women foolish enough to be out in such a storm. When she got into town, it was quite dark; the street-lamps gleamed with faint, quivering reflections along the wet pavements, and the people were pushing and jostling, in their haste to reach the cheerful shelter of their homes.

Elizabeth found herself thinking of the fireside and her mother's face. She was weary of herself; she wanted to escape from this strange triumph of defeat; for, at last, she knew, without reasoning about it, that she was going to accept the facts as they were, — she was going to be happy, and let Oliver be happy. Joy had been hiding itself under the pain of the thought that Oliver might never regain the past. She knew now that she did not want him to regain it. *He loved her;* — and she was glad.

She did not go into the sitting-room when she reached home; she was too wet, she said, standing in the doorway, and smiling at her mother and aunt; tired, but with delicate color deepening in her face, and with the rain still shining in her soft hair, all roughened by the wind and curling about her forehead. "I'll go upstairs and put on some dry clothes, and then come down and set the tea-table," she said; "and

I 'm sorry I 've been out so long, mother dear."
There was a little burst of joyousness in her
voice; yet all the while she was wondering
whether a reaction would come, and she would
find herself capable of taking up her sacrifice
again. Then she saw the letter which her
mother, in smiling silence, held up to her. Mrs.
Sayre's look turned her back into her old reserve; she would read her letter alone.

"I will be down in a moment and set the
table," she repeated, and, taking the letter, she
slipped out into the chilly darkness of the hall,
and up to her bedroom.

It seemed to Mrs. Sayre, waiting impatiently
for news, that Elizabeth took a long time to
read her letter. "'Liz'beth 's like you, Susy,"
she said, "she can't hurry." Indeed, the pause
grew so long that Susan offered to go upstairs
to see what detained 'Liz'beth. Susan was
sensitive about her niece's slowness, because
Mrs. Sayre always pointed out in this connection Elizabeth's resemblance to her aunt. "Do,
Susy," Mrs. Sayre assented, "and tell her we
want to hear what Oliver says." But Susan,
when she returned, looked troubled, and did not
bring any news of Oliver.

"'Liz'beth 's lying down; she says she has a
headache. Dear me! I hope the child hasn't
taken cold, Jane? Don't you think you 'd better give her something hot to drink?"

Mrs. Sayre's solicitude banished instantly all thought of Oliver; she went bustling up to her daughter's room, full of tender anxiety. But Elizabeth, lying white and still upon the bed, would only assure her, faintly, that she was tired; that her head ached; that there was nothing the matter with her; that she didn't want anything. "Oh, nothing! *Nothing!* Only let me be alone, mother; and — and perhaps I shall sleep. Oh, won't you *please* go?" Distressed and worried, there was nothing for Mrs. Sayre to do but kiss her daughter, resting her soft old hand upon Elizabeth's forehead, and stroking her hair gently, with little murmuring sounds of love, and then slip out of the room, closing the door quietly behind her.

When she had gone, Elizabeth Sayre rose, with sudden, violent haste; she slipped the bolt of her door, and then fell upon her knees at her bedside.

Mrs. Sayre knocked gently a few hours afterward, but there was no answer, and she said to Susan that Elizabeth must be asleep, and sleep was the best thing for her; so she wouldn't disturb her by going in to see how she was. She meant to let her sleep in the morning, too, she told her sister-in-law. But when she went down to breakfast she found her daughter in the sitting-room. Elizabeth answered all her mother's inquiries, and kissed her gently, assuring her that she was quite well. A headache was of no consequence, she said; yet it made her absent-minded, and she did not talk very much. Breakfast was almost over, Mrs. Sayre told her son afterward, before Lizzie remembered the great piece of news, and said, with a sort of start: —

"Mother, Mr. Hamilton writes me to say that he is very happy. Fanny has promised to marry him. Tom is very much pleased, and I — I am so glad for dear little Fanny."

AT WHOSE DOOR?

I.

WHEN Friend Townsend's sister married the son of a man who had been known to be a rascal, the whole Townsend connection deplored it with him; and they added to their sympathy the flattery of surprise. Mary was not headstrong, they said, nor restless. She had come of generations of Friends, and that she should marry David Dudley's son was something of which they would not have thought her capable. Among themselves, to be sure, some of the connection recalled a time when Friend Townsend himself had caused them a little anxiety; but that was long past, and then, too, he was a man, and that made all the difference in the world. So Mary's conduct in marrying Henderson Dudley was as puzzling as it was deplorable.

True, the young man did not in any way resemble his father; so far as any one knew, he was honest; and inasmuch as he was diligent in business, and unwilling to live upon his wife's fortune, he might be said to serve the Lord; furthermore, he had never cared to look upon that bad side of life in which David Dudley had found his greatest delight. But he was one of the world's people, and — he was his father's son! This was enough to keep a commiserating sympathy with Joseph Townsend fresh in the minds of Mary's relations, even after she had apologized by dying, and Henderson himself, three years later, had gone meekly out of the world in which he had walked very silently and blamelessly, leaving Mary's child as a peace-offering to his brother-in-law.

Little Rachel was not a Townsend, Joseph's dovelike wife used to say; the spark in those fierce dark eyes, dimmed by sudden despairing tears, or dancing in mirth which "was not convenient," confused and perplexed Sarah. It was inconceivable to her that a child who could lightly disobey her could feel the love which Rachel sometimes protested. Nor could she reconcile a frankness that was often cruel with an insincerity which was almost untruthfulness, not realizing that the one might spring from that ignorance of suffering which is part of the glory of youth, and the other from a desire to say a pleasant thing or a longing for approval. Each day of Rachel's childhood had been full of contradictions. She would wound her aunt by disrespect, and then fling herself upon the ground to kiss a pebble Sarah's foot had touched. She would strike a servant, but cry until her great brown eyes were almost blind because she had found a dead bird in the garden.

The child loved Love. And yet this, her strongest characteristic, denied itself daily with pretense of hate, with furious angers, with sudden disobediences. But had they been read aright, these things were only the outcries and pleadings for love. When Rachel went sullenly to bed without kissing her aunt good-night, it was a pity no one guessed her passionate wish that Joseph's wife should care enough about the kiss to demand it. When she ran half way to town trying to overtake the carriage, though she had been bidden to stay at home, it was a pity no one knew that it was to say, "Forgive me for looking cross; oh, I love thee, aunt Sarah!" But of course no one knew it, for when her disobedience was discovered, the grieved rebuke, and the declaration that it was deceit as well as disobedience, closed Rachel's lips to her confession. Yes, yes; it was a pity, nothing more. Sarah's deep and pathetically intense desire to do her duty to the child kept it from being anything more than a pity. No one could blame her, this quiet, righteous, anxious woman, who saw the child's bitterness with all the uncomprehending dismay of a sweet, cold, untempted soul. It was a pity, too, that Sarah and Joseph had not had children of their own; the companionship would have been much to little Rachel, and doubtless her uncle and aunt would have given less thought and prayer to her training had there been others to claim their anxiety and their discipline, and so she would have been less conscious of her own shortcomings, — and very likely there would have been fewer shortcomings. Certainly other children would have made her aware of Sarah's and Joseph's love for her, and taught her, too, to express her love for them in language they could understand.

"Sometimes, Joseph, I think she has not even natural feeling for us," Sarah Townsend said, as they sat together in their still parlor one September afternoon. The wide, shining top of the mahogany table was between them, but they were not occupied with books or writing. Friend Townsend was nervously pulling to pieces a blossom which had fallen from the bunch of white-winged sweet peas in Sarah's bosom, and his wife's hands were folded placidly in her lap.

The shutters in the long French windows were bowed, for at midday it was still warm on the south side of the house, and three thin streaks of sunshine fell across the drab carpet,

and touched the brass claws on the feet of the
table, and struck a glint from the andirons in
the empty fireplace.   There were no vain and
unnecessary adornments in this room; two sil-
houettes in narrow gilt frames hung high above
the black wooden mantelpiece, and on a rotund
chest of drawers covered with a plain linen
cloth, stood a jug filled with early goldenrod;
there were shelves on either side of the fireplace, full of books in sober bindings, but there
was no warmth of color in all the bare, plain
room, and no pleasant disorder of home life.

Sarah Townsend's sweet face was still young
in its serenity, though the hair beneath the delicate fold of her cap was as gray as her silvery
gown.   Joseph's dark eyes smiled as he looked
at her.

"She must love thee," he said; "don't thee
get discouraged about her, Sarah, or I don't
know where the child will end."

"I cannot be discouraged," she answered with
grave simplicity, "for she is in the Lord's hands.
Yet, if she would but trust us a little more; if
she would believe that we desire only her own
good! She would know that if she cared for us,
Joseph."

"Does thee think," he said, after a moment's
pause, lifting his dark, thin face from his breast
and wrinkling his forehead restlessly, "does thee

think that we trust her quite enough? If we explained to her why we were unwilling that she should see a play, it would be less wearing to us than her perpetual questioning, and it might be better for her to have her judgment agree with ours."

"But is it not best that she should learn the habit of unquestioning obedience?" Sarah asked gently. "She ought to believe that we know what is wise for her without any explanation."

"No doubt thee's right," Joseph assented quickly, throwing himself back in his chair with a sigh; "it is not best to give reasons to a child. · But, Sarah, suppose, instead of forbidding it, we let her go? She would learn, as I did, how empty all such amusement is, — what hunger of the soul it leaves! But to realize that, I sometimes think one must see it for one's self."

"See it for herself!" Sarah said, clasping and reclasping her delicate hands, her even voice trembling a little; "why, Joseph, does thee understand what that means? 'Shall one touch pitch and not be defiled?' Thee knows I do not mean to be narrow. Many of the world's people do go to plays, and they are pious people according to their light; but we have more light. Shall we let the child do wrong that she may feel the misery of sin? Ought we not to save her such knowledge while we have the power

and the right to restrain her? Oh, Joseph,
though thou didst learn to love peace through
thy temptations, remember thou art a man, and
thou wast born a Friend, too. But think of
her father, and her grandfather! Remember
her impulsive, ill-balanced nature; think what
the effect might be."

"Yes, thee's right," Friend Townsend said,
after a pause. "Thee's always right. But I
can't see why she should want to go so much.
It isn't as though she had ever gone, and knew
the pleasure of it. Is it because young Roger
Livingstone asked her? Does she like to be
with him, Sarah?"

"I think it is because we do not wish it,"
Sarah answered with a sigh, "and perhaps be-
cause she knows we do not approve of Roger
Livingstone. It is nothing deeper."

II.

The garden in front of Friend Townsend's
great gray house had been touched by frost,
though the days were languid with slumberous
September heat; the more delicate plants stood
with limp, pallid leaves and hanging heads, but
salvias blazed inside the box borders, and zinnias
were in coarse and riotous bloom. There was a
scent of decay and dampness in the still air, in

spite of the flooding sunshine, and now and then a leaf floated slowly down from the thinning branches of the tulip-trees, through which came the distant flash and ripple of the river.

Rachel Dudley stood leaning against the old sun-dial at the foot of the garden, her chin resting on her hand, and her straight black brows gathered in a sullen frown.

She could not be seen from the house, for the laburnum hedge hid that part of the garden, but any one passing the stone gateway might have caught a glimpse of her slender figure through the osage-orange trees which bordered the dusty turnpike. And Roger Livingstone was watching for her, as he made his horse walk past the line of Friend Townsend's estate; so he was quick to dismount and throw the bay's bridle over the stone ball on one of the ivy-covered gate-posts, and then open the tall iron gate, and hurry down the steps into the damp stillness of the garden.

Roger and Rachel had known each other for many years, but in spite of perpetual quarreling it had never occurred to Roger to fall in love with her, — at least until very lately, and then only because his father had looked at him one day with shrewd good-nature and said: "Remember, boy, the pretty Quakeress has a fortune of her own."

That had made Roger think; but, after all, could a fortune give a man happiness, if the girl was first jealous and then indifferent, and always quick to take offense? Roger thought not; but he liked Rachel, and while he was making up his mind he was involuntarily and unconsciously more friendly. A young man cannot contemplate marrying a girl, even as a remote possibility, and avoid, in his most ordinary conversation with her, a betrayal of the attitude of his mind.

After these careless words about the pretty Quakeress and the fortune, Roger found a new pleasure in meeting Rachel; but he felt, vaguely, that Friend Townsend did not like him, and so he fell into the habit of seeing her oftener in the old garden than in her uncle's house. In these meetings, he did not speak to her of the happy interests of more worldly youth. He could not talk of this harmless diversion or of that pretty folly, a ball, or a dance, or the hundred gayeties that belonged to their years, because Rachel knew nothing about them. The only thing that he could give or that she could receive was sympathy for what she chose to consider the loneliness of her life.

Roger knew that this sympathy gave her pleasure, so, being a good-natured fellow, he was willing enough to condole with her. Furthermore, the half secrecy of their meetings here in the garden, or along some shadowy path beside the river, had a charm for him, to which his father's hint had added a pleasing excitement of uncertainty as to his future sentiments towards her. He was eager now to know if his plan of taking her to the theatre on Saturday afternoon could be carried out.

"Well?" he said, as he reached her side. She glanced up for a moment from under her frowning brows at his handsome, boyish face, as he stood striking at his riding boots with his switch and waiting for her reply.

"It is no use, they won't let me go," she said, gloomily, not even lifting her chin from her slim brown hand.

He turned sharply on his heel, his spur grinding down into the damp moss of the path. For an instant he was too much disappointed to speak.

"It's outrageous!" he cried, "upon my word, it's outrageous! They're cruel, I tell you, Rachel, they're absolutely cruel!"

"They don't care," Rachel said briefly.

"I'd go, anyhow," Roger continued angrily; "why on earth should you give up everything to please people who don't care anything about you anyway?"

Rachel winced. "I know they don't," she said.

"Well, then, make up your mind to go," Roger ended; "it isn't as though they had any reason for saying you shouldn't. Of course, in any reasonable thing, I wouldn't advise you to — to disobey them. But this is folly, Rachel. Honestly, I believe I'd go!"

"Of course it is not *reasonable*," Rachel cried passionately. "Why, if they would give me a good reason, I wouldn't say another word. They just tell me, 'It isn't best,' and if I say 'Why?' aunt Sarah says, 'Thee must trust thy uncle and me.' Trust them!" and she laughed, "they won't let me go because they want to disappoint me. I will trust them to do that!"

"Why, they make a business of being disagreeable to you, don't they?" Roger condoled, his flash of boyish anger gone.

"They think it makes people good to be disappointed," Rachel said, with that contempt which seems to youth so withering. "And they want to make me good, they think I am so wicked. Oh, I am — I am! but if they thought anything good of me I could be good, it seems to me; or if they loved me the least bit, I would not mind giving up everything in the world for them, everything! But they don't care whether I am alive or dead!" She laid her cheek down on the hot face of the dial and sobbed.

"Don't cry," Roger said sympathetically; "what good does it do to cry? Why don't you just go, anyhow? I believe they'd respect you more if you had a will of your own. And it isn't as if they were your own father and mother, you know."

She shook her head. "Oh, I can't! Thee knows I can't. And it isn't that I want to go to the theatre so very much, Roger. If they had only said I shouldn't, differently. It's the way they said it. As though I was wicked to want such a thing; a kind of despair about me; and yet as if, after all, it was only to be expected of me. I might as well live up to it. I might as well be as bad as they think I am!"

Her quick transition from grief to anger dried her tears. Roger did not know what to say; his somewhat slow mind could not keep pace with her sudden changes, and her gusts of feeling wearied him.

He glanced at his horse, cropping the grass about the gate-post, and rubbing his velvety nose against the reddening ivy leaves.

Rachel noticed his look and feared he was going to leave her. "I believe thee's right, Roger," she said. "I believe I ought to live my life in my own way, to make them respect me. I *will* go!"

Roger looked at her with admiration, yet

there was a little doubt in his voice as he said: "It's the only thing to do, Rachel; only — of course — you don't want to make them *very* angry?"

"I don't care how angry they are!" she cried; "it isn't as if they loved me."

"Or as if you loved them," Roger said. "Only — think it over, Rachel. I don't know; somehow, I don't feel quite sure."

"*I* feel sure," she answered, striking her hands sharply together; "but, oh, I do love them — I do! I do! And they don't want my love!"

Roger tried awkwardly to comfort her, but he felt as though he would rather give up the theatre than have any more tears, and he began to think he had been rash to urge her to go.

But Rachel had decided. There was a bitter joy in making herself as bad as her uncle and aunt thought her.

"They expect me to be disobedient; they are always watching for it; so I'll go, Roger!"

III.

It was not, however, quite easy to go into town on Saturday.

"Why does thee start so early, Rachel?" Sarah Townsend said, as her niece put on her

little drab bonnet immediately after the noon
dinner; "thee will have a long afternoon in
town. I wish thee was not such a gad-about.
I wish thee loved thy home."

"Thee will not miss me," Rachel answered,
with the bitterness of premeditated disobedience. She was already beginning to feel remorse, and was blaming her aunt for her suffering. "If thee thinks I am a gad-about, aunt
Sarah, I don't see how thee can expect me to
love my home. I don't see how I can."

Rachel's fingers trembled as she smoothed
the gray ribbons under her chin. But Sarah's
quiet sigh, as she said, "Thee need not try to
show me how little thee cares for thy home, — I
know it too well," was like wind upon the fire.

Rachel flung back some sharp untruth as she
opened the white front door and let herself out
into the sunshine. But there was a sob in her
throat, and her eyes were stung with unshed
tears which blurred the spray of salvia she
stuck in her dress. "I won't look any more
like a Friend than I can help!" she said hotly,
as she picked the flaming blossom, knowing how
such a thought would wound her aunt. But she
did not need the salvia. Her vivid face was not
in harmony with her quiet bonnet and gown;
she looked like one of the world's people mas-
querading as a Quakeress.

Roger watched, with a growing fascination, her kindling eyes and her half-like tears and laughter as the play progressed. He even wondered, as they left the glare of the theatre and came out into the soft dusk of the autumn afternoon, whether he was not very much in love with this strange, wild, pitiful creature, whose restless, throbbing life beat against the calm of her home.

In his uncertainty, and his pleasure in her pleasure, and the charm of stolen excitement, he was almost tender to her, — very kind to her, Rachel thought. He could not help telling her, too, how lovely he thought her face was, "and those little soft rings of hair, Rachel, round your temples, are so pretty!"

Rachel grew scarlet. No one had ever said such a thing to her. She trembled a little, and looked at him with such beautiful, appealing eyes, that Roger said more of the same nature. He spoke of the happiness it was to be near her, and how much he hoped that in the future she would not forget him — ("Forget thee? Why, Roger, I have known thee all my life. How could I forget thee?" she said, simply) — and he observed that life for him had not much to offer now. He *had* loved, but that was in his youth. There had been a girl once — But he would tell her about that some other time.

He would only say now that he had suffered as few men ever had suffered — (though "she" was entirely unworthy, as he afterwards discovered when she married some one else). But that was all in the past, he told Rachel, and he felt that the ashes of memory might kindle again if she would but be his friend.

Upon reflection, afterwards, Roger felt that all this had been very unwise. Not that he had committed himself in any way: on the contrary, he had given Rachel to understand that although his heart, buried in those ashes of memory, was capable of being kindled, it was with no warmer flame than friendship. "But girls are so silly; they're always misunderstanding things," he thought guiltily. And so there were times during the next week, while the remembrance of this indiscretion was fresh, that he tried to undo his words by being a little less than friendly; such an attempt, however, was always followed by a burst of pity for her, and then admiration, and then something strangely like tenderness. As for her, every word he so rashly said that afternoon went deep into her heart, and no temporary coldness in him could make her forget them.

In the excitement and pleasure of the play Rachel lost sight of everything else. Her gladness made the whole world seem loving and lovable.

"Oh, Roger," she said, "it was beautiful! Let's come again."

"We can come every Saturday afternoon, if you only will," he answered eagerly, "and it will be better each time, and Friend Townsend and your aunt will see that it does n't do any harm."

Rachel's face fell. "I had forgotten them," she said. And when Roger left her at the sundial, and she hurried through the garden to the big, silent house, there was no defiance in her heart; nothing but frightened dismay and penitence.

The lamps were not lighted in the hall, only the faint September twilight struggled in through the fanlike window over the front door, but Rachel could see the disapproval on her aunt's face. Sarah Townsend was standing on the lowest step of the staircase, waiting to speak to her niece, before going into the dining-room to see that the candles were lighted for tea. She was fresh from her simple toilet-table; in the clear, fine folds of her kerchief were some rose-geranium leaves, and the spotless muslin of her cap rested upon the shining smoothness of her gray hair. Her exquisite, fragrant neatness was in sharp contrast to Rachel's flushed face; rebellious curls were blown across the girl's eyes and above the brim of her bonnet;

her shawl, too, was awry, and she had torn one glove as she tried to pull it off.

"I hoped," said Sarah gravely, "thee would come out by an earlier train."

"I told thee I was coming at five," Rachel answered, with the quick thought that perhaps her aunt had missed her. "If thee had told me that thee wanted me, I"— Then she stopped abruptly, realizing that she could not have come before. "Why did n't thee tell me? Thee knows, aunt Sarah, the only thing in the world I want to do is just to please thee!" Confession was trembling upon Rachel's lips.

"I want thee to want to come, Rachel," Sarah said simply, and then with her gentle footfall she went into the dining-room, and standing at the narrow sideboard, with its slender carved legs and inlaid doors and drawers, she began to light the candles in four tall candlesticks. Rachel followed her, with that feeling of aggravation which comes when trying to talk to a person who is walking away from one, and with an instant resolution to be heard. Sarah had lighted a spill at the blue flames of the apple-wood fire, and was slowly touching the candle-wicks with it. Its delicate glow shone on her serious face. She looked up at Rachel.

"At least thee knows it does not please me to see thee so untidy," she said.

"Of course thee thinks I would n't have come if thee had said thee wanted me," Rachel cried; "and I could n't help the wind blowing."

"If thee cannot speak respectfully thee can at least be silent," Sarah answered calmly. Then with her quiet step she again passed the girl and went into the parlor, grieved in her kind, just heart at the antagonism in Rachel's voice. And Rachel, in her small, orderly room, gave no thought to repentance, but lived over again the excitement of the afternoon, and Roger's kindness in taking her, and the sound of his voice in those new words he spoke. "I *will* go again!" she said to herself. And she did.

IV.

The miserable consciousness of deceit cannot be entirely escaped even in the height of enjoyment, and the theatre never seemed so pleasant to Rachel again. Indeed, except that it gave her Roger's companionship, upon which she was more and more dependent, she would not have cared to go; and even his companionship did not persuade her more than two or three times, after which her efforts to escape the stings of conscience were very apparent.

Remorse began to stain all her interests, and even her few pleasures. Remorse is a very dreadful pain to the young. They have not the experience of years of wrong-doing to teach them that there will come times of ease from that weight and ache below the breast-bone, that sick feeling of remembrance intruding upon their happy and forgetful moments; still less can they grasp the relief of hoping that remorse may end altogether. Rachel, for mere pain of her sin, sinned again to forget the pain. She was only happy with Roger, but the last expedition to the theatre left her more unhappy than before. She was strangely restless; she took long walks alone, simply for occupation, or hurried into the city and out again for no other purpose than to divert her thoughts from her disobedience. She went over and over in her mind terms in which she might confess what she had done — for it would be such a relief to confess! But the thought of her aunt's dismay, which would have in it no surprise, made the child shrink back into herself.

Sarah Townsend saw the restlessness with concern, but she could have no conception of its redeeming cause. Yet it was not until one November afternoon that she spoke of it to her husband.

"I have not wanted thee to think less well of the child than thee does, Joseph," she ended anxiously, "and so I have not told thee that I was troubled about her; sometimes I think thy judgments are almost harsh, because thy ideal is so high. But it shows such unrest, this running about so much. She ought to wish to be at home. Home is the Lord's place for a modest young woman; it is an unregenerate and shallow mind which demands constant recreation."

"Yes, yes, that is true," Friend Townsend answered. He rose, and began to walk nervously about the room. "It must be stopped," he said. "We must remember her heritage from her grandfather, and insist upon a quieter life and a contented mind. I am glad young Roger Livingstone has gone in town. Sarah! thee does not think she sees him there?"

He paused beside her chair in sudden anxiety.

"Oh, Joseph, no!" she cried, "how can thee think of such a thing! It is only the restlessness of youth which seeks any occupation but duty. A woman of thy family could not so forget herself." With all its gentleness, there was a calm pride in Sarah's face as she said this. "But we must stop her going into the city so much; that impulsive, inconsequent nature of hers must be trained to self-control. Will thee speak to her, or shall I?"

"Oh, thee, thee," Joseph said. "But, Sarah, why did thee not put a stop to it long ago?"

"Because," she answered, sadly, "there are

so many commands to give. I have to reprove
her so often. She does not know how much I
dread to find fault; and she is so ready to be
angry! It seems to alienate her, too, and make
her more unloving, when I do admonish her.
She cannot see that it is only because I love
her that I do it, — but thee knows I love her,
Joseph?"

The wistful tremor in her even voice gave her
husband a shock of pain.

"She has an evil nature," he said angrily, "if
she can bear to make thee grieve."

Yet, as they sat waiting for Rachel to come
home from a long walk in the cold, gray afternoon, his heart melted toward the child; and
when at last she entered the quiet room, he rose
and left it, though in a silence she thought
stern. By himself in the hall, he struck his
hands together with a gesture strangely unlike
his usual calm. "Poor Rachel," he said, "poor
child!" His head sank upon his breast as he
walked restlessly about. Joseph Townsend was
remembering many things.

Rachel was in a softened mood when she came
into the parlor. In her walk along the river
path she had been thinking that, after all, life
might be very beautiful if there were love in it;
— and Roger loved her! She was sure of that.
Yes, a girl might be very glad to be alive, if

there were love in life, and one tried to be good,
—and she meant to be good hereafter. Of
late she had been living in a dream of Roger,
into which the real man had not entered. She
had not noticed his efforts at commonplace
friendliness, for they were so genuine there could
be no sting in them, and beside they alternated
with that talk about 'friendship' which is such
subtile love-making. It needed something sharp
to pierce the mist in which her own construction
of his looks and words had wrapped her. That
afternoon, in the glow of content about her heart,
she forgot for a little while her remorse; and
when she remembered it all, her contrition was
subtly pervaded by her joy.

"Rachel," Sarah said, in her low, even voice,
glancing at the girl, who stood resting her forehead on the edge of the mantelpiece and idly
unfastening her bonnet, "thy uncle and I feel
that thy taking such long walks, and going so
often into town for no purpose, is but idling
away thy time, and we think it best for thee to
put a stop to it. We need not discuss it, but
just remember what I say."

Rachel did not speak, and her aunt, thinking
it was sullen acquiescence, added, "It is for thy
own good; we are sorry to cross thee."

The pleading in Sarah's tone touched the child;
an impulse of love and repentance and happiness

sent the tears brimming into her eyes. "Oh,
aunt Sarah," she said, "I won't do anything
thee does n't want me to, but — but — I have;
and I am so sorry!"

Sarah Townsend looked up at her with sudden tenderness and hope. "If thee is really
sorry it will be easy for thee to please us, my
dear."

At that unusual, almost unknown word, Rachel's reserve gave way. She flung her bonnet
on the floor and sank upon her knees beside her
aunt, hiding her face in Sarah's lap. It seemed
to her that she had begun her confession; and
she was already comforted, and restored in her
own eyes; she did not realize that confession is
relief, not remission.

"It is n't just the going in town," she said,
her voice shaken with tears. "I have done
wrong, aunt Sarah. Oh, I have been so wicked
— so wicked! Thee can never, never, *never*
forgive me!"

Scenes like this seemed to Sarah Townsend
to lack genuineness. It was not necessary to be
dramatic. "Thee must not throw thy bonnet
on the floor, Rachel," she replied calmly, "and
thee must be more composed. Instead of crying, just make up thy mind to be a good girl."

But Rachel could not check her impetuous
remorse. "I did not think it was really wrong

when I did it. I do not believe I stopped to think at all. Oh, aunt Sarah, aunt Sarah, I am so wicked! I have been going into town and — and — meeting Roger, and " —

Sarah put her hands on the girl's shoulders and lifted her with a sharp push.

"What does thee mean, Rachel?" she said.

At the change in her voice, Rachel knelt upright, brushing her hair back from her startled eyes, and looking wonderingly at her aunt.

"What does thee mean about Roger Livingstone?" Sarah repeated, with something which was almost terror in her tone.

"Oh, aunt Sarah," the girl faltered, trying to hide her face on her aunt's knees, but held back by the relentless hands, "I have been to the theatre with Roger, that's all."

"All!" Sarah exclaimed, half with relief and half with indignant protest.

"Yes," Rachel said, covering her face with her hands and sobbing; "yes, that's what I went in town for, three afternoons last month."

Sarah could not speak; she felt almost faint. She did not see that Rachel had put her heart into her hands for good or ill; only the deceit, the disobedience, the dismay at Roger's influence, pressed upon her. She bent her sweet, stern face upon her breast and groaned.

Rachel shivered. "Oh, I am so sorry, — I

am so sorry. I will be good after this, *always*.
I will be good!"

"Perhaps thee cannot be good, Rachel," Sarah said in a broken voice, speaking involuntarily her thought that it might be that the child was not altogether responsible for this warped moral nature; and that perhaps, too, her own severity, which had seemed a duty, had but made things worse. "Thee has deceived us as well as disobeyed us," she said sadly, and paused, but Rachel did not speak; "and thee can find pleasure in the companionship of such a man as Roger Livingstone, — thee, Joseph's niece!"

Rachel rose, the softness frozen, the tenderness bitter. "I have deceived thee, but I am sorry. I have asked thee to forgive me. I am sorry. I don't see what more I can say." She had that feeling, — which often comes with confession, — that by confession the sin is atoned for; and with it a sense of injury, almost anger, that her listener should feel surprise or grief. She resented Sarah's dismay as unjust and cruel. "I've told thee about it; I don't see what else I can do," she said sullenly, tying the fringe of her gray shawl into knots, and never lifting her eyes to her aunt's face. "There is nothing wrong in being glad to see Roger. If he'd been welcome here, I need n't have seen him anywhere else, and — and — I like to be with Roger."

Sarah looked at her for a moment without speaking; then she said abruptly, "Rachel, has Roger asked thee to marry him? I ask thee, though I am not sure that thee will tell me the truth." Sarah was quite calm now, but her mind was confused between distress at this foolish defiance, and the far deeper grief of the girl's deceit. Rachel's lips parted and then closed again. She hung her head in silence.

"Answer me, Rachel."

But Rachel could not speak.

"Does thee mean," Sarah said incisively, "that thee cares for a man who does not care for thee? And that, to be with him, thee has been willing to deceive and disobey thy uncle and aunt? — thee has taken a lie upon thy soul? Rachel, I have known that thee did not love us, and did not cheerfully obey us, but I never knew that thy heart was filled with deceit, and that thee had not the modesty of the young women of thy family. Does thee think we can ever trust thee again?"

Rachel stood without any words, trembling and panting like some wounded animal. She had no thought of self-defense; it was only pain.

"Thee may go to thy room," Sarah said after a long silence; "thy uncle and I will try and decide what had best be done."

Without a word Rachel turned and fled out

into the hall and up the stairs. She caught a
glimpse of her uncle walking calmly up and
down between the tall white lilies in Sarah's
conservatory. He would have to be told! She
scarcely seemed to breathe until she reached
her own room, and shut and locked the door,
and then leaned against it for support. Her
heart was pounding in her throat; her eyes
were blurred and stinging, but without tears.
She heard the parlor door open and close, and
knew that Joseph was listening to the story of
her guilt.

"I cannot bear it!" she said aloud; "no; no;
I cannot bear it."

A gleam of joy came to her in the thought
that it could not be borne; it meant escape from
intolerable pain, though she could not yet see
by what means. Her mind even darted forward
to contemplate a time of peace, and she vaguely
thought of a day when she should look back
upon this misery — But no, it was too terrible
ever to be looked back upon! Pity for herself
made her sob aloud, and without knowing that
she was only choosing the lesser anguish she
began to say, "It is all because they are angry
about Roger." She could not face the truth, that
her pain and theirs was because of her deceit.
It was a little easier to say, "They are angry that
Roger should care for me." By and by a means

of escaping from pain by action began to grow
clear to her. She would go and tell Roger. In
her proud, innocent heart, Sarah's assertion that
she cared for a man who did not care for her
left no sting, save the bitterness that her aunt
should have said it.

"I'll tell Roger," she said over and over
again to herself, for his very name comforted
her.

V.

The warm, fragrant air of the conservatory,
and the silent beauty of Sarah's stately lilies,
had made Joseph Townsend less restless. He
almost forgot his anxiety about Rachel, and
when he came into the parlor he was greatly
startled and alarmed to find his wife hiding her
face in her arms upon the table, her quick
breath showing that she was in tears.

"Tell me, Sarah!" he said. But it was some
moments before she could speak, and then she
said brokenly: "Joseph, Rachel has been de-
ceiving us. She has confessed it, though she is
not really repentant. Think how we have failed
in our duty to her, if such sin is possible in the
poor child!" Then she told him, faltering with
grief and shame, of the deception; but, with a
tender instinct to spare Rachel, she said nothing
of what she felt to be the girl's infatuation for

Roger Livingstone. After all, that was the least important. "But, Joseph," she ended, "think how far we have let her drift from us, that she *could* deceive us! Oh, I have sinned in this; it is my fault — not Rachel's. She does not love us, after all these years, but it is because I have been unworthy of the charge of one of His little ones!"

He tried to comfort her and tell her she was wrong, but for once the brave, silent woman was broken; she would not listen, and by and by went to her own bedroom, pacing up and down the floor in despairing condemnation of herself. Her heart ached for Rachel, yet it did not occur to her to go and comfort the child; indeed, she would have felt it wrong to have seemed to excuse the sin too readily; but, even had it occurred to her, it was too late.

Rachel's vague purpose of telling Roger had assumed a definite form. There was a train into town that she could take which would make it possible for her to see the young man before he went out for the evening. And she would tell him all about it, and he — he would tell her how to act! She had a confused thought of finding a place to board and some work to do, but underneath this purpose was the wordless conviction that Roger would take care of her. She did not think, "He will ask me to marry him;" she only felt it.

At last she rose from crouching against the door, and with trembling little hands put on her dove-colored bonnet, and folded a soft shawl about her shoulders. Then she opened the door and stood for a moment listening, her eyes dilating and her breath coming quickly. There was no sound except the faint snapping of the fire in one of the lower rooms. The hall was quite dark in the early twilight, and the shadows hid her as she crept downstairs; her fingers shook when she turned the big brass knob and opened the front door. In another moment she had closed it stealthily behind her, and stood alone in the gray chill of the November evening.

She looked back once, when she reached the foot of the steps, not hesitating in her purpose, nor with any relenting tenderness, but with the habit of a love which has been repressed and misunderstood. The blinds had not been drawn, and she could see Joseph sitting with his gray head bowed upon his hand; his spectacles were folded across the pages of a book which was upon a little round table at his side; Sarah Townsend's white knitting-work lay just as she had put it down when she began to reprove Rachel; the room looked so warm and peaceful, her uncle sat so quietly watching the fire, his face hidden by his hand, that a wave of bitterness swept

over the child. "What does he care if I am.
unhappy?" she thought; "as soon as the lamps
are lighted he 'll read again." Oh, if they only
had loved her — she already thought of her life
with them as in the past — she could have been
so good! but they would never trust her or love
her again! For an instant she forgot that her
anger was for Roger's sake.

She turned and ran swiftly through the garden; her dress caught on the broken branch of
a rosebush, and she stopped to loosen it, prick-
ing her slender fingers till they bled. She found
herself suddenly crying; it was snowing softly,
and she was cold, and everything hated her.

The rush and tumult of the flying train
drowned her thoughts. She was half dazed
when she reached the city, but in the short ride
to Roger's rooms she began to think how she
should tell him her story. Again and again she
reached a certain point in it, and then seemed
to wait for his answer: "What ought I to do,
Roger? I 'll do whatever thee tells me."

She was so sure of his sympathy, and so ignorant of human nature, that it was impossible for
her to imagine the dismay and almost repulsion
with which Roger, entering his small library
from his bedroom, saw her standing in his doorway, flushed and panting and almost happy.

After his first two terrible words of astonish-

ment there was absolute silence for a moment.
Rachel's color wavered and ebbed, the terror
stole back into her eyes. Without a word of
explanation the enormity of her mistake fell
upon her.

"Has any one seen you?" Roger said; and
then he drew her inside and closed the door.
"For Heaven's sake, why are you here? Has
anybody seen you?" His fright at his own responsibility made him angry. Rachel's beautiful dumb eyes entreated him to understand her.
"Something has happened, I suppose. Tell
me. Oh, Rachel! you should not have come
here. Did you go to my office first?"

"They have found out about my going to
the theatre," she answered at last, slowly. She
had forgotten that it had been her own confession. It seemed to her that she had been
trapped into telling her aunt. "They are very
angry, and they will never trust me again.
Aunt Sarah said she would never trust me again.
So I am going to earn my own living; and I —
I thought thee could advise me — but never
mind."

The pitiful quiver in her voice touched Roger,
but it was chivalry, not love, that it aroused.

"Rachel, dear," he said simply, "I will take
care of you always. You must marry me, Rachel."

But it was too late. With the first look of horrified surprise on Roger's face the woman had been born in her. She scarcely seemed to hear him, and went on speaking as though he had not interrupted her. She was conscious only of a desire to hide from him that she had depended upon him. "I mean to do some kind of work. I don't know what, yet. But I can't live at Uncle Joseph's any more. So I thought — if thee could tell me some place where I could board — I have a little money — But thee need n't trouble, Roger."

Roger drew a long breath. After all, it would never do. It was folly to have asked her to marry him; and Rachel had had too much sense to notice his words.

"Why, of course I 'll help you, Rachel," he said, in a troubled way; "only, honestly, I don't see how I can. Why, Rachel, don't you understand? It would n't do."

"Thee need n't trouble," she said again, vaguely.

"But it is n't that it is any trouble," he explained. "You know I would n't care how much trouble it was, only, what would be the use? You could n't support yourself. Why, my dear girl, what can you do? And, don't you see, Friend Townsend would simply find you, and take you home again. He has the

legal right." Roger was still young enough in
his profession to feel its awe. "Indeed, Rachel," he continued, for she did not answer, "it
was foolish to come to me — to come in town, I
mean; and it was a mistake to think you could
take care of yourself. I know the world, my
child, and you don't. Do go home, Rachel,
right away!"

The old simple friendliness made him very
much in earnest.

"Very well," she said.

"Won't you start to the station at once?"
Roger said eagerly. "Your carriage is at the
door still, and you can be at home again in an
hour. I mustn't go downstairs with you: it
wouldn't do, don't you know. But if you'll
just slip out quietly, nobody will see you, and
they need never know at Friend Townsend's
that you came here."

"I shall know," Rachel said, hoarsely.

"What?" cried Roger, impatiently, but without waiting for her answer; "you can say you
came in town on an errand and missed your
train, or — or anything! But go — go!"

In the sudden fear that some one might come
in and find her there, he was again growing
angry with her folly.

"Yes; I'll go," Rachel answered.

"You see, I don't want any one to know that

you came here to see me, Rachel dear," he explained, relenting with honest sympathy for her mistake, "because, you see, it isn't — well, it isn't usual for a girl to go to a man's rooms, don't you know. So you won't mind my not going downstairs with you?"

"No, I won't mind," she said, looking absently about the warm, bright little room; "I won't mind; oh, no. And I'm sorry, Roger; and it isn't thy fault. Only — I ought not to have been born, thee sees. I — I think it isn't anybody's fault, after all."

"What isn't? What do you mean?" he said, with sudden anxiety, for she seemed so indifferent to him and his explanations that Roger felt a thrill of tenderness.

But Rachel had gone. He followed her into the entry, where the one small jet of gas flared and burned bluely for a moment in the draught from his open door, but she did not look back. He leaned over the balustrade and saw her gray figure hurrying down the coil of the broad staircase, and he stood there, straining his eyes into the darkness and full of troubled pity, until, in the lower hall, the front door opened and then closed with a dull, distant jar.

VI.

And Rachel? The idea of going home again
never presented itself to her, yet, with a dim
consciousness of a promise, she went blindly
towards the station. She forgot the carriage,
although it had begun to snow steadily, and in
her hurried uncertain walk she stumbled once
or twice. The second time a group of men,
who had sought shelter in a doorway, laughed
loudly, and one of them shouted a name into
ears too innocent to know that they were in-
sulted. She turned and looked at them with
the wondering thought that any one was happy
enough to laugh, and they were silenced.

Again the short, swift ride; again the glare
of the lamp outside the little station, the panting engine, the clouds of steam, and, through
all, the beating snow and the gusts of wind.
The station master did not recognize her, and
when he looked again for the one passenger
who had gotten out of the train, she had van-
ished.

She left the road, which ran between leafless
hedges, and, climbing down a gravelly bank,
hurried across a field towards the river. "If
I can only just be quiet and think," she said
again and again; "if I can only be quiet."

She walked aimlessly about the wide, white

meadow, trying to silence the tumult in her
brain which seemed actual noise. She even put
her hands up to her ears once, and stood still,
repeating, "I must think." After a while she
tripped upon the twisted root of a locust-tree,
and, through sheer exhaustion, did not rise, but
sat leaning against its rough trunk. "I'll
think now," she said to herself, and hid her face
in her hands, for the darkness and the storm
began to terrify her. One word, repeating and
repeating itself, had made this clamor in her
mind.

"Oh, yes, yes," she said, as though answering it, "yes, I will die; I must; but I don't
know how. Oh, if God would only kill me;
He might be as kind as that! I have always
been so unhappy, and it would be such a little
thing to let me die! But I have prayed and
prayed, and yet I go on living. Why can't He
let me die instead of some sick person — who
has friends?"

As this thought worked itself out in her
mind, she heard, above her own sobs, and above
the soft, swift rush of the river, the far-off
rumble of a train of cars.

Then, suddenly, it all came to her, how easy
escape was, how simple! A great calm settled
down upon her. She lifted her face with a be-
wildered smile. The snow had caught in the

wet tangle of her dark hair, and blew against her small, pitiful lips with faint, cold touches. Here was the way out of all the pain; she need not pray for it to come to her; she could take it.

She rose, steadying herself upon her tired feet, and began to walk back across the field towards the railroad. She found herself wondering why anybody was alive when it was so easy not to be. She laughed, under her breath, to think how she had prayed for escape when all the while the river had been slipping by, and this other way invited her. And then her mind fastened upon the idea that she was dying for some one else, some unknown, dearly loved sick person. A curious pagan instinct of giving a life in exchange for a life, sprang up in this moment of primal simplicity into which her soul slipped at the thought of death. She would die, and some one else should live. The passion of sacrifice entered into the thought of death and hid the pitiful selfishness of her purpose, a purpose which was only childish impatience with present pain.

When she reached the steep embankment again, she took off her bonnet, and, with the hardly acquired habit of care for her clothing, folded her shawl about it, placing them beneath a tree. Then she climbed the gravelly slope and stood upon one of the tracks; the snow beat in her face, and the wind twisted her wet skirt about her ankles. Again, far back among the hills, came the rumble of the approaching train; she felt the jar under her feet, and then, through the white blur of the storm, came the muffled glare of the headlight.

In an instant the desire for death was swept away. Her instinct to escape pain had been only love of life in disguise. She leaped back upon the other track. "Oh, I did n't mean it, I did n't mean it!" she cried hoarsely. The riotous wind swept her frightened voice like a feather into the darkness, and as the cars rushed past her down the track she stood white and trembling, saying again and again: "I don't want to die, I don't want to die; I did n't mean it!"

She had forgotten — or perhaps she did not know — that the other express was due. The two trains thundered by each other, and left only darkness and the beating snow.

.   .   .   .

If only the great silence could have explained her to them!

"She took her own life," Sarah said briefly; "the child of our old age could not love us enough to live for us. And it was my fault."

"I drove her to it — it was my fault," Roger Livingstone said, under his breath, divided be-

tween grief, and fright, and passionate gratitude that no one but himself knew of the inter-
view in his rooms that last night.   But this
terrible conviction faded and he came after a
while to think, very honestly, that he had loved
her, and she had refused him.   "She would
not listen to me when I asked her to marry
me!   Oh, if she had cared for me I could have
saved her, and now she has broken my heart!"

"It was my fault, it was my fault!" Joseph
Townsend said; "I ought to have understood
her.   We tried to make her good in our way,
when she had a right to her own nature.   But I
ought to have understood!"

A FOURTH–CLASS APPOINTMENT.

I.

THE post-office at Pennyville was at the foot of the long hill up which Main Street climbed a little way, and then stopped as though to take breath and look back upon itself. After that, the street melted into a country road which wandered between the fields, and down the hill to the river and the ferry, and a half dozen houses which were only occupied during that part of the year in which summer visitors invaded the Pennyville quiet. The houses along Main Street stood close together in a friendly way, and ignored as much as possible those scattered on the other side of the hill. Pennyville acknowledged that the summer residents had a certain value, but it looked down upon them as one does look down upon merely useful things. It found some slow amusement in their "airs," and it was rather interested, too, to talk over their various extravagances.

But really Pennyville cared little for the summer residents, and the summer residents cared less for Pennyville. The village was small, — forty houses, perhaps, beside the tavern, which was frequented by occasional drummers with sewing machines or gum boots, and traveling photographers who exhibited enlarged crayon heads; and the dentist, who came twice a year. The houses were built on very much the same plan: a story and a half high, with an entry which was narrow, and generally so dark that one could not see the pattern of the oil-cloth, which was an advantage if the oil-cloth was shabby; and each house had a shed at right angles to the kitchen. All the best rooms had the same cold, shut-up smell, — perhaps because the narrow windows were not often opened, owing to a tendency to stick, which sometimes kept them shut from one spring-cleaning to another.

It was the custom in Pennyville to keep the parlor closed, except perhaps for the sewing society or for a funeral. But, all the same, it was furnished with the best the household possessed. It generally boasted a centre table, on which, standing on a wool mat, there was apt to be a large lamp which waited an occasion important enough to be lighted; — an occasion was so long in coming that the oil was thick and yellow in the red or green glass bowl.

There was, however, one house on Main Street which had a peculiarity of its own, and gained

thereby a certain importance. This was Mrs.
Gedge's, and the peculiarity was a small square
building of one room attached to the house by
means of the woodshed. As for the house, it
was like everybody else's, but that single square
room, over the outer door of which was a weather-
beaten sign, "U. S. Post-Office," distinguished
it and its occupants from all the rest of the
world. The office was quite at the foot of the
hill, before the open green of the common. The
street bent a little to come close up to its door,
so that the stage-driver could hand in his mail-
bag without leaving his seat; that done, the road
bent back, and curved off along the bank of the
creek, crossed a shaking wooden bridge, and
disappeared behind the shoulder of a hill.

Within, this small building at once confessed its purpose; it was divided by a partition,
in the middle of which was a delivery window
surrounded by rows of pigeon holes. There was
a counter in the room, too, and some shelves,
which held immemorial green pasteboard boxes,
whose corners were strengthened by having strips
of linen pasted neatly along each angle. There
was writing paper in these boxes, pale pink and
yellow, with fine blue rulings, or perhaps a picture in the corner of each sheet. There was a
very small showcase on the counter, in which
were tarnished bits of jewelry pasted upon

yellowing cards, and some scent bottles, and
bottles of red and blue ink, and, of course, the
sober black as well; but that was less popular.
The contents of the showcase had been so long
familiar that, with the exception of the ink and
pencils, no one ever thought of purchasing them.
Standing on the scratched and dim top of the
case were three jars which held red kisses and
white, little hard gumdrops, and fat black sticks
of licorice.   There were two or three posters
on the walls of county fairs, or of the traveling
bell-ringers; one as recent as within two years.

In the middle of the room was a small air-
tight stove with a chair beside it.   "I would
have more chairs if it was mine, this post-office,"
said Mrs. Gedge, "but it is a place for business, not sociality; so the government don't
provide chairs, and it ain't for me to seem to
criticise by bringing in any of my own."

Mrs. Gedge and Amanda had lived in Pennyville all their lives, and in the social life of
Main Street had held their unassailable position; but since these pigeon holes had been
put into the small, detached room which once
held Adam Gedge's cobbler's bench (twenty
years ago now), — since that time, Mrs. Gedge
and Amanda had grown vastly more important.
They were the custodians of the United States
mail; they were intrusted with public moneys;

they had mysterious communications with Washington; it was reported, although carefully not asserted by either mother or daughter, that they had had a letter from the President! The consciousness of their obligations and responsibilities clothed them as with a uniform. Amanda Gedge carried her tall, angular form with a precision suited to the parade-ground, and walked with a military tread. Mrs. Gedge had been known to put an end to a political discussion which had begun around the stove while she was sorting the mail, on the ground that she was "connected with the administration, and it was not right, to her mind, for her to be present when it was criticised. So, if they pleased, they could step outside and talk about it." Lord Salisbury could have no better excuse for refusing to discuss the Queen's speech.

That was eight years ago, when Mrs. Gedge was able to sort the letters herself, and hand them out of the little window in the middle of the pigeon holes, and so could not help overhearing comments upon the weather, or the church, or, once in four years, the politics of the nation. But now that pleasant and important task was over; instead, she sat all day long behind the partition, with her crutches beside her, and her knitting in her crippled old hands, while **Amanda** took her place at the delivery window.

Amanda was a trifle deaf, and, when in her official position, very much absorbed by her duties,
so that she did not often notice the discussions
carried on in the open space about the stove,
which space, Mrs. Gedge admitted, belonged
to the Public. Then, too, although Amanda
appreciated her position, her deepest thought
was always for her mother, and she was not so
apt to reflect upon what was due to her official
personality as to think anxiously of Mrs. Gedge's
health, or to plan small pleasures for the little
frail old woman. Still, she knew her importance, as a representative of the United States
Government.

It was all pathetically genuine. Amanda's
severe bosom had thrilled with the purest patriotism when, twenty-four years before, her father
had enlisted. With him had gone Willie Boyce.
Willie had come home a year later, too sick to
give much thought to his old sweetheart, and
only able, his mind fastened on his own suffering, to grope wearily through a few months of
wretched living.

Adam Gedge had never come home again.
Amanda did not know her father's grave, but
Willie's was over on the hill. It seemed to
belong to Amanda, for the young man's family
had moved away from Pennyville, and left him
to her. More than that, the poem on Willie's

gray slate headstone had been the one great achievement of Mrs. Gedge's life, — she had composed it, but it only; genius had never burned again. Amanda sometimes felt that her father's death had been the price of the post-office appointment which had come to Mrs. Gedge in '64, and so she was a little more gentle with the Public than was her mother. Official life, Mrs. Gedge had been heard to complain, did sometimes make one seem severe. And yet so little had greatness really hardened her heart, so patient was she with the well-meaning Public, that she had several times illustrated the pa-ternal side of government by small indulgences, such as delaying the mail-bag for a letter which she knew was being written by a slow but anxious correspondent. It was quite an ordinary thing, too, for her to give a stamp to a customer who had chanced to leave his purse at home, and when he remembered his penny debt, he was always silenced by magnanimous refusals to recognize such paltry obligation; the deficiencies caused by such governmental generosity gave Amanda many arithmetical difficulties, and lessened their already slender income. But neither Mrs. Gedge nor Amanda begrudged that; they liked to be kind to the Public, they said to each other. Their inconvenience was *noblesse oblige,* and to hold back the wheels

of government was but the consideration of the
powerful for the weak.   Yet such is the in-
gratitude of that capricious body which they
so indulged that there had been more than one
irritated protest heard in the open space before
the delivery window.   To be sure, such protests
had always come from the summer residents,
"and," said Mrs. Gedge, comforting her daughter, whose elderly face was flushed, and whose
eyes glittered with tears, "you really can't expect anything else of such people, Amanda!"

"Well, I must say it was unreasonable,"
Amanda agreed.   "Mr. Hamilton knows that
we have to consider the Public, but he says *he*'s
the Public, —and only here six weeks in the
summer!   I told him, said I: 'Mr. Hamilton,
Mrs. Dace wanted to send off some collars she'd
been making for her daughter, and I knew she
only had a stitch to put in them.   If I'd sent
the mail-bag down by the morning stage those
collars wouldn't have been in it, and Mary Dace
wouldn't have got them in time for Sunday.
So I kept back the bag, and coaxed Olly to take
it down on the evening stage.'   Well, Mr.
Hamilton was just as unreasonable!"

"You shouldn't argue with those people,
'Mandy," objected Mrs. Gedge.   "The Govern-
ment is the only thing you've got to consider.
If Mr. Hamilton don't like the way the Govern-

ment serves him — well, let him carry his letters
himself!"

"And it was nothing but a paper that was
delayed, anyhow," Amanda explained for the
third time.

Mrs. Gedge pulled her knitted shawl comfortably around her shoulders. "Of course we do
sell more stamps when they are here — the summer people — but they are so fussy and over-
bearing, even to us, that I don't think they are
worth the money they bring in. I declare, I
believe they think Pennyville belongs to them."

But a sense of importance will sustain one
under small irritations, and so these annoyances
did not really disturb the peaceful life in the
little old gray house. All that summer, which
was tremulous with the excitement of the great
campaign that was to come, Mrs Gedge sat
tranquilly behind the pigeon holes with her
knitting; or, when it was too damp to be
wheeled through the shed to the post-office, had
her chair pushed beside the kitchen window
so that she could see the stage draw up to the
door for the mail-bag, and watch the Public
come and go. The kitchen was such a pleasant
room that, save for the anxiety of feeling that
Amanda was bearing alone the burden of official
responsibility, Mrs. Gedge would have enjoyed
her days there. When it began to grow cool

in September, Amanda potted her geraniums
and put them on the shelves in one of the south
windows, where they flourished so finely that
one did not have to touch the vigorous leaves
to notice their faint musky scent. Amanda
kept the stove bright with a cheerful glitter of
polish, and the worn "two-ply" in the centre of
the well-scrubbed boards gave a hint of comfortable color underfoot. Over a little table
draped with a crazy patchwork cover were some
bookshelves, which held the Bible and "Pil-
grim's Progress," and one or two such faithful
friends; but scarcity of books left more room
for the few ornaments which Mrs. Gedge had
long loved, and which Amanda revered because
she had known them in her childhood. A
whale's tooth and a bunch of wax grapes are
not awe-inspiring perhaps, but no age or famil-
iarity can rob them of beauty if they have ever
worn it to childish eyes. There was a small
flag in a china vase on the top shelf, and
there was a chromo of General Grant over the
pantry door. The most striking expression of
the love of country, however, was the shed
door, which opened on the square grass-plot between the house and the post-office. Adam, the
night before he had marched away, had, in the
fervor of his patriotism, run over to the paint
shop, and begged from Silas Goodrich three

pots of paint, and then, while Amanda and
Willie Boyce stood and watched him, he painted
the door in alternate stripes of red, white, and
blue. At first Mrs. Gedge was proud of it, and
was careful, as the paint began to flake a little,
to have it renewed; but a half-dozen times in
the last ten years she said she would have that
door painted a nice drab. Amanda's non-acqui-
escence, however, — it was never more positive
than that, — still kept the colors of the Union
bright.

"You know you did n't see him paint it, mother. You were upstairs. But I saw him," she
said, her mild brown eyes vague with memory.

"Yes, yes," Mrs. Gedge assented, growing
reminiscent. "I was upstairs sitting on the
cowhide trunk, crying. You know I wanted
him to take his things in your grandfather
Beed's cowhide trunk, and he said he could n't
take a trunk. My, how I cried when he said
he could n't take a trunk! It seemed so poor,
and I did n't give up asking him to do it until
the last minute. And oh, how I felt, seeing
him go without a trunk! It was a presentiment,
child. You were too young — only eighteen
— to feel it as I did. You did n't cry."

Amanda's eyes blurred at the thought of her
mother's grief. "No, I did n't cry in those
days," she said. "I did n't seem to have time

to cry. I just followed him round and round, and I saw him paint the door. But you were always a pretty crier, mother."

"Willie Boyce stood there beside you, too," Mrs. Gedge went on. "I can see him to this day. He wasn't pretty, Willie wasn't, but that never seemed to make any difference to you. Poor Willie! He was buried with his folks; that must have been a comfort to him. Many's the time I've wondered whether he knows that I wrote the poem on his tombstone? It would please poor Willie."

But that mention of Willie Boyce turned Amanda silent. She said she must run over to the office, and left her mother wondering why the child never would talk about her beau; and so again the question of the painting of the shed door fell into abeyance. "Though, being a flag, as it were," Mrs. Gedge insisted to herself, as she sat before the winking embers of the stove, "it does seem to bring our position in the Government right into our private life."

II.

By October of that year even Pennyville had stirred in its satisfied indifference, and was hearing the voice of the nation instructing and suggesting and contradicting itself. The voting population listened, with a sort of slow amusement, to the men who came to tell them that their party had outlived its usefulness, and to entreat them to "save the country." In all these years Pennyville had never been so near holding political opinions. It was really very interesting. Even Mrs. Gedge said that if they were true, — the things that were said about the party in power, — she hoped Government would turn them out; but she regretted this indiscretion afterwards.

"It is n't for us to express an opinion, child," she told Amanda; "though, of course, they are all anxious to know what we think."

Amanda made some vague reply. She was less interested than usual in her own greatness. These October days brought the anniversary of Willie Boyce's death, and her mind kept wandering to that mound over on the hillside. She remembered, with a wonderfully pitiful love, his weary indifference to her in the weeks that he lay dying. "Willie was sick," she said to herself many times, and never thought of being hurt; it only made her love him more. But no doubt her abstraction made her less careful about the letters; she dropped one on the floor at the midday distribution, and did not notice it until evening. Then she slipped a shawl over her head and ran across to Mr. Goodrich's with it.

"It's lucky it wasn't for that Hamilton man," Mrs. Gedge asserted, rather contemptuously; "he'd have made a fuss about it, you can better believe."

As for Silas Goodrich, anything so important as the arrival of a letter made the delay of an hour or a day a very small matter; it had come, and that was all he cared about. He never dreamed of finding fault.

The next day was the day that Willie Boyce had died, and in the afternoon Amanda went up to the graveyard with a wreath of immortelles, which she had dyed pink and blue and vivid green. She leaned it against the slate headstone, and then knelt down, and with her handkerchief carefully wiped a piece of glass set into the slate to cover a faded tintype of a consumptive young man in a soldier's uniform. Amanda looked at the picture long and wistfully. Some day, when she had saved the money, she was to pay ten dollars and have a crayon copy made of this tintype. She had decided to do this a dozen years ago, when a traveling "picture man," passing through the village, had suggested it to her. Ten dollars is not a large sum to save in twelve years, and it had several times been reached, but just as the last dollar or dime was added to the little fund, there was always some call for it. Her mother needed a wheeled chair, or a new cooking-stove must be bought, or the re-shingling of the roof was absolutely necessary; and so the cold closed parlor of Mrs. Gedge's house was still without a crayon.

Amanda, kneeling, picked away some dead leaves of the myrtle on the mound, and then scraped a flake of lichen from the inscription. She knew the lines by heart, but she always read them over with unfailing pride for her mother as well as tenderness for Willie.

"William P. Boyce," it ran, "died for his country," and then the date, followed by the verse which Mrs. Gedge had composed:—

> " Oh, traveler, whoever you may be,
>   Take warning and advice by he
>   Who lies beneath this tomb.
>   He went to war and died,
>   And now in paradise is glorified.
>   Mourned by his friends."

"Mourned by his friends," Amanda repeated; and then she stooped and kissed his name.

After that she went home. She was very silent that evening, and her mother was full of small devices to cheer her. She told her how Mr. Hamilton's John had come down to see whether a letter he expected in the noon mail might not have been overlooked.

"He said that Mr. Hamilton expected it

yesterday. I told him no, of course it hadn't
been overlooked. Such a time about a letter!
Well, he's gone, anyway, Mr. Hamilton has.
I wonder he didn't stay over until to-morrow
to get his letter."

Mrs. Gedge did not mind the severity of her
sarcasm if only 'Mandy would cheer up a little.
("My goodness, and her beau dead nearly
twenty-five years!")

"Yes," she proceeded, "he got a telegraph,
—a man on a horse brought it, —and then I
saw him driving off like a crazy man. Those
summer people have no sort of consideration for
their beasts; he made those horses fly."

Amanda looked uneasy. "I don't think I
could have missed his letter," she said; "but I
guess I'll just run over and give a look into the
bag. Don't you remember that time Mrs.
Ainn's letter stuck in the bag?"

She took a lamp, shielding its clear flame
with a large bony hand as she walked through
the draughty shed to the post-office. The mail-
bag, lean and empty, hung between two chairs,
awaiting the morning letters. Amanda put her
hand in it and felt all around. "Of course
there's no letter," she said to herself, indignantly. "It's just as mother says, they do
fuss so!" She stopped to see that the fire was
quite out in the stove, and then, with the severe

smile with which she always tried to check
levity unsuited to the place, she opened one of
the candy jars and abstracted two gumdrops.
"There! I guess mother and I can have some;
they're getting stale." And as they had been
purchased in June, Mrs. Gedge accepted the
extravagance and indulgence with but little
protest.

Afterwards, looking back upon it, that evening seemed to Amanda Gedge wonderfully
pleasant. She set the table and made the toast
and tea, and her mother told her she might get
out a tumbler of gooseberry jam as a treat;
after the dishes were washed, they sat down by
the stove, and while Amanda mended her stockings Mrs. Gedge talked. These two quiet
women found life very interesting. First, of
course, was the consciousness of their own importance, which naturally suggested much conversation. Then, too, they had all their past
to talk about, which, to be sure, had had its
sorrows: little Charles, who died when Amanda
was ten years old; Willie Boyce,— though it
was only Mrs. Gedge who talked of him; and
the soldier-cobbler, whose grave had never been
tended by wife or daughter, but which, somewhere in the South, was marked "unknown."
They could speak, too, of their happiness in not
being obliged to draw a pension. "Government

gave us our position, so we are independent," said Amanda. And Mrs. Gedge acquiesced, and said that a pension would have made her feel like a beggar, *anyway ;* but not needing it, being in the Government, it would make her feel like a thief to have it! Then they could talk of the geraniums; their looks as compared to last year, or the year before, or many years before; and the frost; and how long the tub of butter was going to last. Yes, life was very interesting.

The next morning it rained, and was too damp for Mrs. Gedge to go through the shed; so she settled herself at the kitchen window for a long day's knitting. The stage came swinging and creaking down the hill, and the four horses, sleek and steaming with the rain, stood, with much pawing and jangling of traces, in front of the post-office, while the young red-faced driver, knocking with the handle of his whip on the off wheel, called out: "Good-morning, 'Mandy. Mail ready?"

A moment later Mrs. Gedge saw Amanda hurry out with the still lean bag in her arms, and hand it up to Olly Clough to put under his feet on the toe-board. Olly flourished his whip, nodded, went jolting over the bridge, and disappeared behind the hill. Mrs. Gedge could not imagine why Amanda should stand there bareheaded, her gaunt shoulders covered only with a little square blue-check shawl, apparently forgetful of the rain. She scratched upon the window pane with her knitting-needles to attract her daughter's attention, but Amanda did not seem to hear her, although she turned slowly and went back into the office. It was certainly ten minutes later before she came through the shed into the kitchen.

"Why, what kept you, child?" demanded Mrs. Gedge, whose curiosity never flagged concerning small happenings.

"Mother," said Amanda, "look at *that!*" She held up a letter as she spoke.

Mrs. Gedge stretched out her hand for it eagerly, and then stopped to put on her glasses, so that, holding it at arm's-length, she might read the address. "'Arthur Hamilton, Esq., Pennyville, Pennsylvania.' Well, child, — but how did it come this time of day? Oh, it was in the bag yesterday, after all?"

Amanda was quite pale; she pushed back a lock of hair from her high bleak forehead. "Mother, do you know, that came day before yesterday. That's the letter he was inquiring after. It got shoved into one of the low pigeon holes. My *goodness*, mother!"

This burst of excitement really alarmed Mrs. Gedge. "Why, child, you needn't be so put out. He ain't in town. And I don't know as I'd send it up to his house, anyhow; if he gets it when he comes home, he'll know it's been delayed, and then he'll fuss about it. I don't believe I'd send it, 'Mandy?'"

"Oh, mother, I don't hardly think that would do," Amanda said. "You know the Government" —

"Well, perhaps so," Mrs. Gedge assented, reluctantly. "Course, I wouldn't think of such a thing if it was anybody else. But that man! and he's gone now, anyhow, and probably he's found out what was in the letter by this time, so he hasn't any need of it; and, you know, he's had no experience; he don't understand how a mistake could be made. Well, I don't see myself, 'Mandy, how you could get that letter into one of those pigeon holes. There, it isn't any matter, child. Send it up with his noon mail."

"No; I must take it," said Amanda, firmly. "I'll have to bundle you up, mother, and wheel you into the office. It'll take me an hour to go and come, and the office can't be shut up all that time."

Mrs. Gedge did not half like it, she said; it was not right for the Government to wait on Mr. Hamilton by carrying him his letters; it was trouble enough to sort them out, she declared; but nevertheless she permitted Amanda to push her wheeled chair through the shed, and place her on the official side of the pigeon holes, within easy reach of the stamp drawer and the letter scales. If anybody wanted gumdrops or writing paper they would have to help themselves, and bring her the change.

Amanda put on her overshoes, which she, like the rest of Pennyville, called "gums," and a rusty black waterproof cloak, which was thin and skinny and soaked up more rain than it shed. She wore a faded straw hat with a barége veil tied around its crown. Her large freckled face was pale, and her anxious eyes looked out from under a forehead that was creased with troubled lines. Clutched tightly in the hand which held her skirts very well up out of the mud, was Mr. Hamilton's letter.

It had rained since before dawn, and the branches of the sycamores and lindens had given up almost all those few yellow leaves to which they had clung since the last frost. The ground on the footpaths was covered with them, and the streaming air was heavy with the dank aromatic scent of autumn. The wheel ruts were full of running yellow water. Amanda picked her way carefully, but her Congress gaiters were soaked above her overshoes, and even the white stockings on her lean ankles were splashed.

She was glad it had not rained yesterday, she said to herself; and then she thought of the wreath of immortelles, and hoped the colors would n't run.   She sighed as she remembered the tintype set into the slate headstone under the piece of glass, which to-day must be so spattered with rain that the young soldier in his uniform could not be seen.   How beautiful it would be to have the black and white crayon! Amanda knew just where it was going to hang on the parlor wall, and she had a plan about a cross of purple immortelles to place above it.

By the time Mr. Hamilton's house was in sight Amanda had gone through a calculation as to how long it would take her, putting aside five cents a week, to save up the three dollars and eighty cents which the required sum still lacked, granting that nothing else came to claim her hoard.   This calculation seemed to bring the crayon nearer, and cheered her, in spite of the rain and the burden upon her conscience.   She hurried up the driveway to the front door, which was opened by John.

"Oh, John," said the postmistress, out of breath and embarrassed, yet holding her gaunt shoulders proudly, and ignoring the way in which her hair, lanky with rain, had blown into her eyes; "John, this letter was — overlooked. You may give it to Mr. Hamilton."

John took the letter curiously. "Well, now! When did it come?" He paused to examine it closely. "Yes, it's postmarked Washington. Why, Miss Gedge, it's the one he was lookin' for two days ago. They had to telegraph him to come on. Lord! he kicked like a steer about it. 'Postal delays,' says he. Obliged to you for bringin' it, miss."

Amanda did not reply; she was gathering her skirts up under her waterproof again, and shaking open her umbrella.

"You might 'a' saved yourself," John protested, politely; "he's fetched up in Washington by this time; so the letter ain't needed, as you might say."

Amanda nodded, and went plodding down the carriage road, her tall body leaning against the wind that twisted the waterproof around her ankles and beat her umbrella over sidewise; the blue barége veil hung wet and straight over one shoulder. A cold misgiving fastened itself upon her heart. "Postal delays." And Mr. Hamilton was in Washington; suppose he should find fault, — suppose it should reach the Government? Not but what the intimacy of their relations with the Government would make an explanation simple enough; but yet it was not pleasant to think that Mr. Hamilton might speak to the President in some unkind way of her

mother.   She wished the President could know
how they revered him.   She had never begrudged
her father and Willie Boyce to her country; she
wished, if Mr. Hamilton did say anything, that
the President might understand all that; but of
course he could not.   Probably Mr. Hamilton
would not think to mention her father and Willie, even if *he* knew about them, and — Amanda
tried to be just, even to Mr. Hamilton — it was
pretty plain that he did not know, seeing that
he was "so unreasonable and fault-finding."

The wind suddenly twisted her umbrella, and
her face was wet with rain; and then something
warm went rolling down her cheek.   She had
not known that she was crying.

III.

When Amanda had put on some dry clothing
she hurried into the office, for there was much
to do before the arrival of the noon stage.
What with her work, and listening to Mrs.
Gedge's minute account of all that had tran-
spired in her absence, she had no time before
the mail came to tell her mother of her anxieties.
Amanda listened to every word of the small
happenings with close attention : Sally Goodrich
had come in for two stamps, and her five-cent
piece had rolled down in that crack by the stove;

but Mrs. Gedge had said, "Never mind, Sally, you can have them just as well;" for it was raining, as Amanda knew, and Sally Goodrich at her age — she was sixty-one, if she was a day — could not go back in the rain just for four cents; besides, the five cents was really in the post-office, and if the floor should ever be raised they'd get it. Mrs. Gedge, having been silent for an hour, talked in a steady, cheerful stream, broken only by Amanda's little interjections of surprise and interest.

But after dinner, which the noon delivery of the mail made sometimes as late as one o'clock, Amanda could not help saying that she wished that that letter had belonged to anybody else than Mr. Hamilton.

"Oh, you take it too much to heart, child," Mrs. Gedge reassured her. "Why, 'Mandy, he's only a summer person; he'll go away, and we won't see or hear of him till next summer, nor his sister either. They're a pair of old maids, the two of 'em," said Mrs. Gedge, with a chuckle, her bright black eyes snapping with good-natured impatience.

"Well, mother, may be that's so," said Amanda, doubtfully, "but Mr. Hamilton's John took the letter, and he seemed to think Mr. Hamilton was dreadfully put out about it. He said that he *kicked.* I suppose he meant that he stamped his foot."

Mrs. Gedge gave her cap strings a jerk. "Well, what if he did? It shows he's a very bad-tempered man, that's all."

"Yes; only — he's in Washington, mother."

Mrs. Gedge did not seem to understand for a moment, and then she suddenly looked concerned. "Well, now, Amanda, how could you overlook that letter? Dear me, child, I don't see how you did it. Why, if he's in Washington, he might say something to the Government. I tell you, I wouldn't like that, Amanda!"

Amanda sighed, and shook her head. "If there was any excuse," she said; "but there isn't. It was — it was the 28th of October, mother, *you* know; the day before the — 29th; — and I was sort of dull. Well, I suppose I couldn't write that to Washington?"

"It's a very good excuse," cried Mrs. Gedge. "I'd like them to know just what excuse we have, if he *should* say anything — but I don't believe he will, 'Mandy — I'd like them to know we didn't mean to be neglectful."

The kitchen had grown dark with rain and early dusk, and a chill had crept into the air in spite of the crackling fire in the stove.

"Well, now, 'Mandy, I'll tell you what would be a good thing; better than writing," Mrs. Gedge said, thoughtfully; "*send a present.*"

"To Mr. Hunter?" said Amanda. Mr. Hunter was the gentleman who signed the occasional communications from Washington, and to whom they submitted their quarterly accounts.

"I meant the President," said Mrs. Gedge, doubtfully, "but I don't know but what Mr. Hunter would be better. Then, if Mr. Hamilton should presume to find fault, Mr. Hunter would know that our intentions were all right."

"Oh, mother, I *don't* know," Amanda demurred. "May be we 'd better not do anything. May be he won't complain."

But Mrs. Gedge was positive. "No; a present is friendly, and he 's probably a busy man, being in a big post-office; so, if he has a present from us, it will be easier for him to keep us in mind as being friendly."

"Well, mother, you 're right, I guess. And yet it seems sort of queer, don't you think? And what could you send him?"

"Oh, I 've thought of that!" cried Mrs. Gedge. "We can send word by Olly Clough to his friend at Mercer to buy an album, — a blue velvet album like Sally Goodrich's, with those steel trimmings and clasps."

Amanda was moved at the prospect, but suddenly her face fell. "Mother, Sally's album cost nine dollars and ninety-five cents," she said.

Mrs. Gedge was dismayed. "Perhaps we need n't get such an expensive one?"

"No; if we get any, it ought to be a handsome one," Amanda said, sadly. "Well, mother, you can may be begin to make the toast for tea, and I'll run over to the office and see if we've got the money to spare."

Mrs. Gedge was quite cheerful by that time, and she chatted merrily all the evening of Mr. Hunter, and his surprise and pleasure at being remembered by humble officers of that Government to which he himself rendered more important but not more loyal service.

"Why, child," Mrs. Gedge said, suddenly, in the middle of supper, putting down the cup she had just raised to her lips,—"why, 'Mandy, suppose I was to write a poem, and send with it?"

Ever since Willie Boyce died, Mrs. Gedge had meant to write another poem, but there had been no occasion great enough to inspire her.

"Well, now, that is a good idea," Amanda answered proudly. "It would be real pretty to send a poem with the present."

And for the rest of the meal Mrs. Gedge tried excitedly to find words that rhymed with Hunter, but they were so scarce, "and not real sensible," she said, that she turned to "album," which was hardly more successful, although it rhymed well enough with "dumb," and "come," but she did not just see what words she could get in along the line. Amanda tried to help her mother, but she sighed once or twice as she heard the rain on the kitchen roof, and thought of the tintype under the misty glass.

The commission was given Olly the next morning. He was to tell his friend, who was, Olly said, "a traveling commission merchant," to be certain, the very next time he came out from Mercer to Pennyville, to bring a blue album. If he could find one that had two flags crossed on the clasp, like Sally's, he was to get it, even if it cost a quarter more. He was to try, however, to find one just as good as Sally's for, may be, a dollar less. Olly was so hopeful that his friend could economize that Mrs. Gedge checked him.

"It is n't the money, Olly, that you consider when you 're getting a present for a friend, it 's the album; it must be the best. It must be as good as Sally's."

After that there were many days of expectation, for no one could tell when Olly's friend would arrive. In Mrs. Gedge's mind, the reason for the present had faded in the excitement of the present itself. It had been easier, no doubt, to forget the reason because Mr. Hamilton had not come home. Indeed, when, flushed with triumph, on the Wednesday following the second Tuesday in November, John came into the post-office for the mail, he volunteered the information that very likely Miss Hamilton would close the house, and join her brother in Washington.

"We'll be there this winter," said John, with an important air, "though of course we won't get to work before the 4th of March."

This news that Mr. Hamilton might not return was a relief to Mrs. Gedge, but still more so to Amanda. She seemed to breathe more freely, for, ever since John's betrayal of his master's temper, she had dreaded a scene with Mr. Hamilton in the post-office. "I'd put him out with my own hands," she had thought, "rather than have mother worried." But the danger was averted, and in her thankfulness Amanda was reconciled to what she had come to think was really a very unnecessary expenditure of money, for Olly's friend would probably not be able to return any change from the nine dollars and ninety-five cents which had been intrusted him.

It was not until well into December that the friend "got around" to Pennyville. When he did, it was a great day at the post-office. He came on the noon stage, and brought a large package with him. Olly handed in the mail-bag at the same time; but no one could think of that until the package had been opened, and the album, covered with rich bright blue plush, very soft and deep, and indented with oxidized clasps, had been displayed and admired. Every one who called for a possible letter was quite willing to wait a half-hour until the excited representatives of the Government were able to attend to their duties. This willingness spoke much for the good nature of the Public, as well as for its patience, for neither Mrs. Gedge nor Amanda confided the purpose of the album. It was "a gift," they said, and with that the admiring and inconvenienced Public was forced to be content. It was curious, where their official relations were concerned, to see the reticence of these two simple women who had not a secret of their own. Their reserve was perhaps the most striking indication of their pride of office.

The people who had not received any mail lingered longest, kicking their steaming boots against the little ledge about the stove, and waiting, as though in the hope that a relenting afterthought on the part of the postmistress might create a letter. But when the last disappointed correspondent went tramping out into the snow, the mother and daughter gave themselves up to the contemplation of their treasure. They took it back into the kitchen, and placed it, with almost reverent care, on the crazy patchwork cover of the table; then they touched the plush to see how soft it was, and studied the pattern on the clasps, and counted the pages. It was a most exciting, a most exhausting afternoon.

Sally Goodrich came in at dusk to have a look at the album. She was a little condescending at first, but its magnificence overpowered her, and she honestly confessed that it was far handsomer than hers. She said that she presumed the person it was for would be real pleased? But the tentative assertion did not flatter the mother or daughter into giving her the information she desired. They were impatient to be alone, that they might compose the letter which was to accompany the gift.

They did not, however, get at it until after tea, and when they did, Mrs. Gedge could not easily resign the idea of poetry; but Hunter was not a name that charmed the Muse.

"'Oh, traveler,'" Mrs. Gedge began, "'whoever you may be'— I could use as much as that of Willie's poem, 'Mandy? Dear! I do hate to be put out just by a name. I suppose I need n't put it at the end of a line, but it seems to come that way in my mind. Hum— hum — hum — Mr. Hunter !"

They struggled over this with patient earnestness before turning to sober prose; but at half past nine a letter was at last composed, and Mrs. Gedge went to bed, weary and happy, appalled at the lateness of the hour, and charging Amanda to be careful of the album. Amanda tucked it up in its box, under a sheet of tissue-paper, as tenderly as though it were a baby. It lay on the table at Mrs. Gedge's bedside, and when Amanda got up the next morning at half past five to make the fire, she found her mother awake, and anxious. for a look at the beautiful book before she arose.

"I can't wait till I get up, child," she said, her eyes, under the full ruffle of her nightcap, bright with excitement and pride.

It was hard to part with the album by the noon stage, but it had to go, and the letter, prim, and full of respectful assurances of regard, went with it. How the thoughts of the contented donors followed it along each step of its journey! Mrs. Gedge was concerned about the weather; she said that she hoped the snow wouldn't drift badly on the hill road; Amanda would remember how Olly's father's stage had upset on the hill road in the great storm? In an accident like that, an express package could so easily be lost, she said, anxiously. She and Amanda calculated the exact moment that it would reach Washington, and the earliest date when an acknowledgment could be looked for.

By this time — mid-December — Mrs. Gedge had quite forgotten Mr. Hamilton. Her life had too many pleasant and interesting things in it to allow her to think about a bad-tempered man, who was nothing but a summer visitor anyhow. Amanda, too, had almost put aside her fear, although the tintype up on the hillside and the vacant spot on the parlor wall were constant reminders that propitiation had seemed necessary. Mrs. Gedge did not admit that the album had been propitiatory; their gift was simply a pleasant courtesy to an equal, for were they not both officers of the same great and beneficent Government? That Mr. Hunter's acknowledgment seemed long in coming could not alter that fact; very likely he was away, or may be there was sickness in his family, as Amanda had more than once suggested. But it certainly was long in coming, for the 1st of January found Mr. Hunter's manners still at fault.

Yet although the post-office had forgotten Mr. Hamilton, Mr. Hamilton, now that the immediate excitement of the second Tuesday of November was over — Mr. Hamilton remembered the post-office.

"I tell you, Philip," he said one evening, as he and a friend sat over their wine after dinner, — "I tell you, the Post-office Department of this country needs a tremendous shaking up. Yes, sir; heads have got to fall. I have a summer house in that little place, Pennyville, you

know, up in the hills, and for all practical pur-
poses there is no post-office there; outrageous
carelessness and endless inconvenience. But I
intend to do my part to secure a proper postal
service to my native land."

"At least during the summer?" commented
the other man. But Mr. Hamilton ignored the
sarcasm.

"There's a good fellow, a good hustling fellow, that I mean to have put there. William
Sprague — you remember? He was my substitute; he has a ball in his leg now that belongs
to me. I'm going to speak to Stevenson, and
have that job given to him. I've always meant
to do something for him."

"Ah, how I respect a philanthropist!" said
his friend; "and how just it is that, because he
was your substitute in the war, the nation should
reward him! And yet I thought that civil service reform was alluded to in your Convention?
Correct me if I am wrong."

"Oh, bah!" answered the other, laughing,
and knocking his cigar ashes off against his
wineglass. "Shore, we've been out in the cold
for twenty-four years, and we don't propose to
keep away from the fire to split the straws of
ethics. You may consider that statement official, my boy."

"Is that the excuse you will give to the pres-

ent incumbent when you tip him or her out? It
will have all the merit of truth."

"Look here, my young reformer," protested
the other man, "I advise you to take off your
kid gloves. These ideas of yours are too
damned fine for our humble capital. Yes, sir;
they will do for Boston, and I am sure we are
grateful that the chaste bosom of the Boston
mugwump should have thrilled for us because
of our highly moral principles; but, my dear
fellow, *now* we have come down to business in
spite of our principles. We are a great deal
more honest than the people you helped us put
out, there is no doubt of that; but we are human. This may surprise you, as you reflect
upon our virtues, but we admit it — human.
And how shall we dispose of the present incum-
bents in Pennyville?" He rose, with a jolly,
rollicking laugh, straightening his shoulders,
and lifting his handsome head. "Why, Lord
bless you! offensive partisanship, to be sure.
Seriously, they are hopelessly inefficient; a
couple of old maids, who hold back the mail-
bags, lose a man's letters, or deliver them a
week after they've arrived. Why, look here;
here's an instance: That letter from the Secre-
tary about the Cincinnati matter was overlooked three days. Thank the Lord, Beardsley
had the sense to telegraph; he knew the Secre-

t.ry had written. Now, you know, that would
have cost me more than it is agreeable to contemplate. I swear it *was* offensive partisanship.
Deliberate injury to a political opponent — if
Beardsley had n't had the sense to telegraph!"
He laughed, and then struck the younger man
good-naturedly on the shoulder. "See here,
Philip, don't, by the fineness of your theories,
make yourself unfit for practical life. Remember what we 've got to deal with. Be as good
as you can, but, for the very sake of your theories, don't be too good. Does n't the Bible say
somewhere, don't be righteous overmuch? Well,
a printed notice of that ought to be sent around
to the mugwumps!"

IV.

"It does seem," Mrs. Gedge said, when, towards the end of January, no acknowledgment
had come from Mr. Hunter, — "it does seem as
though something had happened to that album."

"Well, mother, Olly saw it safe into the express office; it must have got to Washington,
anyhow."

"You don't suppose," Mrs. Gedge queried,
in a troubled voice, — "you don't think he could
have thought it was out of the way, two ladies
sending him a present? It was in our official

capacity, Amanda; I hope I know better than
to do it in any other way."

"My, mother! of course he understands it,"
Amanda assured her. "It's just as I say, sickness in his family, or something, has put it out
of his mind. We'll hear soon. Now don't you
worry; it was a nice gift, and will look pretty
on his centre-table, — you can be sure of that."
They had followed the album so closely with
their fancy that they knew quite well how it
looked. Mrs. Gedge had even said that she
hoped his wife was not a foolish young thing,
who would know no more than to put other books
on top of it, and crush the plush.

Poor Amanda began to dread the coming of
the mail-bag, for each day there was always
the same hesitating question: "I suppose you
did n't hear to-day, 'Mandy? I somehow did n't
look for a letter to-day."

"No, mother, not to-day," and then some
little excuse: "He would have had to write on
Monday to reach us by this mail, and Monday's
a real inconvenient day;" or, "I guess he's put
off writing till the end of the week;" or, "It's
the first of the month, and you know how busy
the post-office is; very likely he's real driven
with his accounts."

But day by day Mrs. Gedge's assurance that
she knew it was all right, of course, and that

she knew, too, in her position, "how hard it was for some folks to write letters," — day by day such assurances grew more evidently forced in their cheerfulness, and when at last the 1st of February passed, and the usual official communication from Washington failed to bring with it any personal communication, Amanda said to herself that she couldn't stand it. They had written to the express office, and learned that the package had been received and delivered, so they could not even have the comfort of thinking that it was lost.

Amanda's high forehead gathered new wrinkles in those bleak winter days, and anxiety gnawed at her heart, for the suspense was wearing upon her mother. Sometimes she thought of writing to Mr. Hunter, imploring him to just say that he had received the present; but how could she deceive her mother, or have a secret from her?

One afternoon, coming home from sewing society, she stopped on the bridge to look into the water, and think. Some uncertain, hesitating flakes were wandering through the gray air, marking the hurrying stream with fine white touches, then fading into its blackness. Amanda's breath caught in a sob. "Oh my goodness, that old album!" she said to herself. Her resentment at the album, which was surely responsible for Mrs. Gedge's feebleness, was only an expression of her own dull ache of apprehension.

The water came racing down the wide, shallow bed of the creek, leaping with tumultuous ripples over the larger stones, and sending a faint continuous jar along the worn hand-rail of the bridge, nicked and whittled by each generation of Pennyville boys. It was freezing, and the ice curved in and out along the curving shore in clear and snowy lines, like wonderful onyx or agate bands. The branch of a maple, dipping into the water, had encased its twigs in a fringe of icicles that jangled as they rose and fell on the current. The cold dusk and the vague, uncertain snow seemed to Amanda the embodiment of disappointment. She plucked a splinter of wood from the rail on which she leaned, and dropped it into the creek, watching it swirl on the black water and go hurrying under the bridge; and then she went slowly home. She had made up her mind to tell her mother that she believed Mr. Hunter was dead. She felt sure that this would be a sort of comfort to Mrs. Gedge, and Amanda was willing to mourn Mr. Hunter, if his demise would excuse his carelessness towards her mother.

She did not propose this solution of the puzzle until the next morning, and then Mrs. Gedge's concern about the Sixth Auditor of the Treasury was almost as alarming as her previous suspense, so that Amanda, with a desperate feeling of not knowing in which direction to turn next, made haste to qualify her suggestion, or even take it back altogether.

The wind was high and cold that day, but the sun shone, and, feeling so much the shock of the suggestion concerning Mr. Hunter, Mrs. Gedge said she believed she would not get up; she said the glare of the sun on the snowy roof of the post-office hurt her eyes, and she'd rather lie in bed.

Amanda's heavy heart grew still heavier. "Mother's failing," she said to herself. "I guess he's well, mother," she assured her. "It was real foolish for me to think he was n't. Why, they'd have sent *us* word if anything had happened to him, of course. I don't know what I was thinking of."

"Well, then, why don't we hear from the album?"

But Amanda had nothing better to say than, "Well, now, I guess we will, real soon."

"You don't think anybody thinks anything, do you, 'Mandy? You never let on to anybody — Sally Goodrich or anybody — that it was for Mr. Hunter, and he has n't written?"

"No, mother; no, indeed. There is n't a person that guesses. Nobody but Olly saw the address, and he don't know who Mr. Hunter is; he don't know but what he's a relation."

There were no demonstrations of affection between these two; it would not have occurred to Amanda to kiss her mother, but she took her little blue check shawl from about her own shoulders and laid it across Mrs. Gedge's feet. "I'll be over from the office as soon as ever I can," she said. She hurried so in sorting the mail that she was not so much as usual on the lookout for a Washington letter, when, suddenly, she found it in her hand. Amanda's heart seemed to come up in her throat; she stopped her work to hold the letter tight in her trembling fingers. It had come! Her mother would surely feel better and get up for dinner. In the confusion of her thankfulness the impulse of prayer spoke in her heart, but she had no words except, "Oh, mother'll get up! she'll feel better!"

"Here's a bundle for you, 'Mandy," said Olly. "I clean forgot to leave it when I hove in the bag."

She opened the delivery window and took the package, but she was too joyfully excited to notice it. She had begun to put the mail into the pigeon holes with one hand, holding the precious letter tightly in the other; she pushed the bundle a little to one side. "It's some

blanks, I guess," she thought. It seemed to
Amanda that Sally Goodrich was never so long
in getting her purse out from the deep pocket
of her petticoat to pay for the sheet of writing-
paper she had purchased; nor was Mr. Thyme,
who kept the tavern, ever so insistent that it
was time for inquiries about summer board, and
he didn't see why there weren't no letters for
him.

In spite of being thus delayed, Amanda was
smiling with happiness when it struck her that
the package was a present from Mr. Hunter.
Oh, this was almost too much relief and joy!
When at last the Public had gone, she seized
the bundle and the letter, and ran through the
shed, the red, white, and blue door banging
after her with great clatter of the latch; but
Amanda could not pause to close it. Oh, the
agitation and joy of these two women! The
rush of forgiveness for having had so many days
of waiting, the joyous excitement of imagining
Mr. Hunter's gratitude, and the wonder and
awe of the accompanying package!

"I hope he didn't feel under any obligation
to give us a present, kind as it is in him. Open
the letter first, and see what he says. Hurry,
child!"

Amanda's fingers blundered with the envelope, and she read in a breathless way. Mrs.

Gedge sat up in bed, and pushed the wide ruffle of her nightcap back, so that nothing might escape her delighted eyes: —

"'Mr. Hunter desires to acknowledge the receipt of a package from Mrs. Gedge, as per letter, for which he begs to express his thanks. He regrets that he must herewith return the package, his position precluding the acceptance of gifts.'"

Mrs. Gedge leaned back on her pillows, with pitiful fright and bewilderment in her face. "'Mandy, it's our album," she said. "Oh, 'Mandy!" Her cheeks seemed to hollow in, and her chin shook. "'Mandy, it's our album!" she whispered.

Amanda Gedge stood breathless. "Why!" she stammered, "why, mother; why, wait! It must be all right. Oh, mother, don't cry!" But Amanda was crying herself. "I think he's friendly; let me read it again. Now listen, mother; he begs to express his thanks, — *begs*, mother. Oh, I'm sure he's friendly. He regrets, — that means he is very sorry; regret means being sorry, mother. And it is his position, the letter says, that makes him return it. And — and he tells the person who wrote it for him to send his thanks, mother.

You see, he's so busy he can't even write himself."

But the shock was too much for Mrs. Gedge to be able at once to see the "friendliness" in the letter written by "another person." She dropped her worn old face on the pillow and whimpered like a child. "Take it away," she said feebly, and Amanda carried the album into the kitchen. She was so excited and frightened about her mother, so angry that Mrs. Gedge's gift should be rejected, that the quiet woman touched the only note of passion that had ever come into her life. She put the album down on the table with something like violence, and then gave it a shove with her bony hands, and said something under her breath. It was nothing more than " *You!* " but Amanda understood the spirit of the Third Commandment as she had never in her placid life understood it before.

It was several days before Mrs. Gedge could look calmly at the album, or consider the letter reasonably, but little by little she began to say that it was "all right," and she believed that Mr. Hunter was friendly. "It's his position, 'Mandy," she explained again and again. "He could n't help sending it back; he told the person who wrote his letter for him to say he could n't help it. It's his position."

Meantime March was blown into April; it

had been a hard month for Mrs. Gedge, with
the excitement about the album and the constant
changes in the temperature. But Mrs. Gedge
was not the only person who found the season
trying. William Sprague said to Mr. Hamilton, who dropped in in the friendliest way to
see him one day at his news-stand in Mercer,
— he told Mr. Hamilton that he felt that old
wound in his leg in such weather; why, he believed that he could foretell a storm as much as
three days before it came, and he said he did n't
know but what he 'd offer his services to the
Weather Bureau in Washington; and then he
laughed, and said he believed it would be an
easy lay, if Mr. Hamilton would excuse his
speaking that way. But Mr. Hamilton would
not let him talk about excusing himself; he said
that he thought William would be the better for
a change; and then he said a dozen words that
left his hearer aghast with pleasure.

"And I 'm to be ready the last of April, sir?
Well, there 's not much to do. I 'll sell out
here, and pack up my duds. I have n't many,
now my poor wife 's dead and gone. I auc-
tioned off most of the furniture; did n't need it,
you know."

William Sprague's face was red with excitement. He was a short, stout man, with kindly,
twinkling blue eyes and a grizzled, rough red

beard. He wore a G. A. R. badge, and walked with a limp and roll; he was stiff with rheumatism, but was never too crippled or too hurried to stop to do a kindness, — pick up a fallen child, and comfort it with a penny, or walk an extra mile to do a favor for a friend. And yet his friends were apt to say he was contrary, and cite as an instance his long feud with McCormick, his rival on the next block, — a warfare waged with the greatest bitterness on Sprague's side, and furnishing much pleasant interest to those not concerned in it.

"William was like to kill him till McCormick got the fever, and then, darn him! he up and nursed him for six weeks. But they're good enemies again now."

William Sprague liked to do a kindness, but it is a question whether he could do a kindness if it were expected of him. "I won't be drov'," said William; and he never was.

"I'll feel bad to leave some of my friends," he told Mr. Hamilton; "but I'm obliged to you, I'm obliged to you, sir. There's nothing I'd like better than to run a post-office. You can count on my vote when you're runnin' for President. Take a paper, Mr. Hamilton; take a 'Herald.'" He folded a paper and thrust it into the hand of his patron. "No, sir, no, sir; not a cent. I guess I can give you a paper; and a good Democratic organ, sir."

He laughed, and so did Mr. Hamilton, accepting the present with gracious politeness, and lifting his hat slightly as he said: —

"Much obliged, Sprague. Well, good-morning. I shall expect to see you settled when I get down to my country house in June." Then he stooped and patted Jimmy, William's rusty little Scotch terrier, and went away.

William Sprague was, as Mr. Hamilton said, a capable, efficient man. He went to work to wind up the affairs of his news-stand in a methodical and business-like manner. He drove a sharp bargain with the man who bought him out, and cleared ten dollars by the sale of odds and ends about his small premises.

"I'd meant to pitch 'em into the ash bar'l," he confided to one of his cronies, "but of course I didn't tell him so. I said I was going to pack 'em up and take 'em along, and of course that made him hot for 'em." He winked and chuckled, and then whistled to a newsboy across the street, and tossed a quarter to him. "Sonny, if you'll bring in a dozen of the fellows to-night, I'll give you a treat."

And he did. "He come down handsome," the boys said, afterwards, with ice-cream — two kinds — and three doughnuts apiece.

The days went slowly to William Sprague, waiting for his appointment, but they passed with placid haste to Mrs. Gedge. She had grown reconciled to her own explanation about the album.

"It would n't have been proper, 'Mandy, for him to accept it. I can see that now. And, 'Mandy, I don't know but what — I thought of it last night, lying awake — I don't know but what we did wrong about that blotter. You know the blotter with ribbons that Sally Goodrich gave us for the office last summer? 'Mandy, it was n't proper to receive presents in our position!"

V.

April was very lovely among the hills. The sunshine, threaded sometimes by sudden showers, and chased by cloud shadows and soft, warm winds, lay like a smile upon the meadows. The lilac buds opened like green stars, and had that faint, indefinable fragrance which the later purple blossoms exaggerate almost into coarseness. The creeks were high, and the whirling brown waters shook the wooden bridges in a threatening way; the red buds of the maples dipped into the flood, and strained and tugged at their stems as though trying to be off on its turbulent freedom; all the world was full of joyous life and promise.

Amanda Gedge went up to the burying-ground on the hill to brush away the sheltering dead leaves on the mound, and plant a root of lilies of the valley. The sky was softly blue and the sun was warm upon the slope, and, although it was indiscreet for a person who was over forty and rheumatic, Amanda, after she had performed her little office of love, spread out her shawl, and sat down on the grass to meditate. Something must be done about the tintype; of course she could not think of the crayon for a year or two yet; but the bit of glass covering the picture on the headstone was so spotted with mildew within, that no amount of polishing on the outside made it possible for her to see Willie's face. Now if she could get that glass off and clean it well? The thought of holding the tintype in her hand after all these years gave her a strange thrill. It was like touching the mysteries of the other world! She would get Silas Goodrich to set it again, for Silas added the profession of glazier to that of painter, plumber, and horse-doctor to the village of Pennyville. The doing this for Willie gave Amanda Gedge a curious joy, the phantom, perhaps, of that happiness she might have known had she been his wife and had the joy of serving him. She smoothed the grass where, under the sheltering dead leaves, it had whitened to a silky smoothness, and she hoped the lily root would grow. Willie had loved flowers, except toward the end; then, one September day, when she carried him a bunch of glowing salvia, he had turned fretfully away, and told her not to bother.

"Willie was so sick," she said to herself, remembering, but remembering only his pain, not his slight. She always said good-by to him when she had to leave him here alone on the hillside. Amanda knew that Willie was in heaven, but somehow he seemed here, too, under the leaning piece of slate and the bleached winter grass.

When she got back to the post-office, a little tired, but full of the peace of the calm, sweet day, her mother had a dozen small and pleasant happenings to tell her. And Amanda listened to everything with keen interest and sympathy, and then confided her plan about the glass, to which Mrs. Gedge cordially assented, although she thought to herself that it certainly was strange for 'Mandy to be so faithful to Willie, after all these years. She did not believe, feeling the way she did, that 'Mandy would ever marry; it was a pity for a girl to be an old maid! Well, she liked to have 'Mandy faithful to her beau. "But," said Mrs. Gedge to herself, "my! what would she have done if she'd been left like me, if she takes on so, and Willie only her beau?"

It was too dark to knit, but she saw Amanda, who was sorting the mail, put aside an official letter, and she was eager to know what was in it. "Do make haste, 'Mandy," she said. "My, I wonder if they are going to make any change in the stamps! I don't want to find fault, but they're not pretty — the stamps."

Amanda looked over her shoulder to caution her mother not to speak so loud, — the Public must not overhear an official criticism! But she took time to give her mother the letter; for, though Mrs. Gedge could not read it in the fading light by the window, and Amanda had both lamps to assist her in sorting the mail, she knew that it was a satisfaction to her mother even to hold it in her crippled old hands. But when her public duties had been discharged, Amanda made haste to open the envelope.

"I can't stop to talk," she said, with her official smile, to two or three women who were waiting to gossip in the twilight, "because I must attend to some Washington business;" and, properly impressed, the ladies were satisfied to talk to each other.

"Read it, child, read it," said her mother, sticking her knitting-needles into their little ivory sheaths.

"'MADAM, — It is deemed for the best interests of the service that a change be made in the post-office at Pennyville. Your resignation will, therefore, be accepted, to take effect on the 1st day of May.

"'Yours truly,   —— ——.' "

The name that followed Amanda did not know.

"Why, I don't understand," interrupted Mrs. Gedge. "Why, what does it mean?"

Amanda stared at her mother; then she grew suddenly faint, and sat down.

"But I don't understand," Mrs. Gedge repeated.

"Mother, don't! they'll hear," Amanda interrupted in a whispering voice.

Mrs. Gedge looked up at her in a sort of terror. "'*Mandy?*"

But, without a word, Amanda wrapped her shawl tightly about the little, old, shrinking figure, and with a swift motion opened the side door into the shed.

"I'm going to wheel mother into the house," she called out to the women who were standing by the counter.

Her voice was husky, and there was the swift precision of agitation in her manner, which they noticed and commented on. They said they supposed that Amanda Gedge was getting real worried about her mother, and no wonder, either. They waited a good while, hoping that Amanda would come back; but as she did not, they said it was lucky they were there, for Mrs. Dace came hurrying in to buy a stamp, and there was a good deal of giggling and chattering about being the postmistress, for, rather than bother 'Mandy, they went behind the pigeon holes themselves, and, in the most obliging way in the world, opened the stamp-box and received Mrs. Dace's two pennies just as well as 'Mandy herself could have done. And then, laughing and making fun, as they expressed it, they went off into the twilight, leaving the old post-office in dusky quiet, with the door standing hospitably open.

It was nine o'clock before Amanda Gedge came back. She closed the door, turned the lamps down low, and dropped into a chair, her head resting in her hands. She went all over the last three hours; her mother's bewilderment and terror; the shock to her pride, a pride which seemed, Amanda had thought, watching the old face wither and whiten, — to be her life; then the struggle to understand, and at last the rally of courage with which Mrs. Gedge cried out suddenly that *she* knew what the letter meant! The relief of her own insight was for a moment almost too great for words. "The best interests of the service," she said, with a gasp. "For our interests, 'Mandy; don't you see? It is just consideration. They think I'm too old for such hard work. That's it, I know it is. It's kindness. But, 'Mandy, child, you go right over to the post-office and write to the President; you tell him I am not too old to work for him. He thinks I am, 'Mandy, — you can see that from the letter, — and he gives me the chance to resign; but you say I am obliged, but it is n't necessary. You see, he don't understand; he's new himself, you know, and he don't understand; he thinks the work is too much for me. Oh, don't let him think I don't appreciate him, but tell him I could not think of it. Why, 'Mandy, you tell him I could not desert the Government after these twenty years! And explain to him how much you are able to do now you are older. You know you were so young when I got the place, and they have forgotten that you are older now; I suppose nobody thought to explain that to the new President." She looked up at her daughter, and actually laughed with relief. "My! it did give me a start! But you see what it means?"

"Oh, yes," Amanda assured her; "why, of course." But she said to herself, "I *don't*

know, I *don't* know. May be she's right.
But we won't resign, anyhow. We won't do
it!" And then she reassured her mother again
in that brief, repressed way that never knew the
relief of a caress, "Never you mind, mother;
it's all right."

But Mrs. Gedge's confidence had not come at
once; there had been a dreadful hour of bewilderment and mortification and terror. And now
Amanda, sitting alone in the dark post-office,
put the explanation aside and faced the facts.

"They will 'accept' mother's resignation.
It's Mr. Hamilton did it. Oh, that man!
Well, we won't resign; that's all there is to it.
We won't resign. I'll write and tell the President so, and very likely we'll never hear anything more about it. But, 'tenner rate, *we
won't resign.*" She would never forgive Mr.
Hamilton, she was sure of that. The blow to
her mother, — Amanda's shoulders shook with
sobs, as she sat there, her head on her knees,
swaying to and fro with misery — the shock to
Mrs. Gedge was too great to be forgiven. "Oh,
if I only hadn't lost his letter!" she said, again
and again. "It's my fault; it's all my fault,
not mother's. I'll tell the President that."

But she must not waste her time; she must
explain that her mother was much obliged, but
did not care to avail herself of the consideration
and kindness of the Government.

This for Mrs. Gedge to read; then on a sheet
of thin pink paper, with a print of a rose in
the upper left hand corner, came her own self-
accusation; she wrote with a tumultuous haste,
unlike her usual labored correspondence with
the department. The words were burning in
the elderly woman's heart. "Oh," she said to
herself, "even if they did mean it kindly, as
she says, it may kill mother."

She sobbed as she wrote; but when the letter
had been sent, and a few days had passed without
any further communication from Washington,
Amanda was calmer than she had thought she
could be while this cruel uncertainty was hanging over her. Mrs. Gedge began to gather an
immense amount of comfort and pride from this
expression of the consideration of the Government. She told Amanda that she really wished
the Public knew of it. She didn't want to be
proud, she said, but it was gratifying, and she
almost wished Sally Goodrich knew it. Amanda's feeling was so decidedly against this confidence that Mrs. Gedge reluctantly gave it up.
"Yes, you're right," she said; "we're not
like ordinary people; we can't tell our affairs."
And Amanda was quick to say that was just
how she felt. But her mother's innocent importance cut her to the heart, and gave her,
too, a sort of terror of the weakness of which

she felt it to be a sign. Although no answer
had come from Washington, and the refusal to
resign had apparently been accepted without a
protest, Amanda Gedge found herself counting
the days until the 1st of May. She did not
know why. She only felt that something was
going to happen then. But those soft spring
days brightened Mrs. Gedge wonderfully, — the
days and the quiet of her mind, for, not hearing
from the President, the shock of the letter she
had at first so grievously misunderstood faded
from her memory. Such forgetfulness only made
Amanda's heart sink.

The second week in April Mrs. Gedge said
that, although she felt better, she believed she
would not go over to the post-office for a few
days; the being wheeled over made her bones
ache, and she 'd just as lief stay in the kitchen,
she said. But of course she kept an eye on the
post-office, and saw the stage come rumbling
up at noon, and watched the off horse pawing restlessly, while Olly handed the mail-bag
to Amanda. There was a man on the box-
seat at Olly's side who roused her curiosity a
good deal; and when her daughter came in to
get dinner, she asked her if she had noticed
him.

"He was real pleasant-looking," she said, as
Amanda pushed her chair up to the table; "real

pleasant, but big; though he ain't to blame for
that. Who do you think he can be? He had
a little dog sitting up beside him, like a little
deacon! I like to see a man friendly with a
dog. He is n't the sewing-machine man; may
be he 's a dentist?"

"Or a book agent," suggested Amanda. "I
like book agents, they have so much conversation. Sometimes I think, really, if I 'd the
money, I 'd buy one of their books, they do
talk so nice about them."

"He looked real hard at the shed door," Mrs.
Gedge commented. "I guess he never saw a
shed door painted just so. I don't know but
what we 'd better change it, 'Mandy?"

"I guess he thought it was nice, mother,"
objected the other, gently.

"Well, anyway, when Mr. Thyme comes
down for the mail, child, you be sure and ask
who he is. It 's far too early for a summer
boarder."

It was delightful to have a new and interesting topic of conversation. William Sprague,
"cleaning himself" before a small mirror in the
office at the tavern, had no idea how much pleasure his advent had given. William's coming
to Pennyville thus early, was simply because
his important happiness demanded some kind
of action. The day that Mrs. Gedge had been

notified that her resignation would be accepted, a communication had come to William Sprague, showing the reverse side of that letter which, as Mrs. Gedge expressed it, "she had misunderstood." He read it for sheer pleasure a dozen times a day, and each day the 1st of May seemed farther off! He packed his trunk at once, and when he had had a week of inconvenience in unpacking and repacking whenever he wanted anything, it occurred to him that the best thing he could do would be to take Jimmy and go to Pennyville at once, and, while waiting for the desired date, become acquainted with his constituents, so to speak.

"It's two weeks before I go into office," he told his friends, "but I'll be learning the ways of the place and the people, so as to get a good grip on the work."

He was as full of enthusiasm, and of plans for reform in what he knew nothing about, as was Mr. Hamilton himself. He took it for granted, after the manner of all new brooms, that everything in Pennyville was in the most shocking condition of neglect and dilapidation. Yes, the sooner he got there and looked about him, and investigated the poor, feeble, inefficient workings of the post-office, the better. And so, with only the delay of carting his trunk to the station, William Sprague hurried off to his new life. He was glad when the journey in the cars was over, and, whistling to Jimmy to follow him, he could clamber up on the stage, and take the box - seat with Olly Clough, and then go swinging and creaking along the hilly roads toward Pennyville.

William Sprague did not tell Olly who he was; he preferred the sensation of coming into his kingdom in disguise. He was very gracious, though; he complimented the country that stretched before him, in terms which intimated a friendly desire to overlook any mistakes on the part of the Creator; he thought the houses looked comfortable, he said, and the barns quite a size; he admitted that it had apparently rained considerable, but he felt that it did good, after all, a big spring rain; it did good, and he would not find fault. By and by he approached the subject of Pennyville.

"Pretty place?"

Olly looked vacant, and said he did not know. "I ain't thought about its being purty," said Olly.

"Large population?" Mr. Sprague inquired.

"Well, sizable," Olly answered.

William Sprague cleared his throat and seemed much interested in the off leader. "Good mare that? Yes? Ha — hum — the post-office, now" — this with striking indifference — "quite a job to run it?"

Olly stuck out his lips to hide a satisfied smile. "Yes, she's fair — she's fair. You don't see none better 'an her in the city."

William answered briefly, but it was some time before he could woo Olly from the subject of the mare, and when he again asked his question about the post-office, the stage-driver was plainly not interested.

"Well, I never heard 'Mandy complain," he said.

"'Mandy?"

"'Mandy and her mother keep it; been there since the war."

"Well!" said William, much interested. "What are they goin' to do?"

"Huh?" Olly inquired. "Do?"

"Why," said William, with some modesty, "when the change is made. You know the other party is in now; they're puttin' in their men."

Olly's low chuckle came as though jolted out of him. "Well, I guess they won't put anybody in our post-office over 'Mandy and her mother." He paused to point out silently the green expanse of the valley below them. Olly thought it was good farming land himself, but the summer visitors always made a fuss about it, and so he had learned to point it out to any passenger on the box-seat.

"Pretty good, pretty good," said William, with absent graciousness, watching a cloud shadow chase across a meadow and up the sloping fields to the woods; "yes, I must say that's pretty fair for these parts."

They rumbled along for nearly a mile without a word, William Sprague feeling vaguely depressed and uncomfortable, when Olly broke out: —

"Why, look a' here. They ain't got a cent, 'Mandy and her mother; ef they were n't in the office, they'd be on the town. Talk about puttin' people in over 'Mandy and the old lady! I guess they'd wish they was n't put in. I guess they'd be considerable put out!" Olly laughed at this joke several times during the next hour. "Put in, put out," he repeated, and chuckled.

But William Sprague frowned in a troubled way. "There!" said he to himself, "I am sorry for the women, but it ain't for me to say anything. I'll do my duty, that's all I'm here for. The women ain't my business. But it's queer they haven't told this young man about the change. I should think they'd tell him, sure; seeing he carries the mail."

He had no inclination now to disclose his identity to Olly, whose ignorance puzzled him, and even irritated him a little, too. But he was quite good-natured again and full of interest and excitement by the time they turned into Main Street and drew up at the post-office. He looked about curiously while Olly handed in the mail, and said in a loud whisper that that red, white, and blue door showed a good spirit. He would not call until he had gone to the tavern and cleaned up, he said to himself. That done, and a comfortable dinner disposed of, he put on his broad brimmed felt hat and went with something of a roll and a limp, and with Jimmy close at his heels, down to the office.

It was three o'clock, and Main Street was quite deserted; the door of the post-office was partly open, and a puff of wind showed its official interior. It showed him also a tall, angular woman standing behind the counter; her back was toward him, for she was trying to fit one of the pasteboard boxes into its niche without wrenching its feeble joints. At his step she turned with rather a pleased look. ("He hasn't a bag, only a dog," Amanda said to herself; "what can he be?")

"Good-afternoon," said William Sprague, taking off his hat, and then putting it carefully on his head again. "How do you do, ma'am?"

"Good-afternoon," returned Amanda, politely. "Fine day, sir."

"Well, yes, it is, it is," William conceded, pleasantly.

"Are you stopping in town, sir?" inquired the postmistress. She was not surprised that he had called at the office; what more important or pleasant place was there? Amanda was always gracious, if a little formal, to people who came to pay their respects. She patted Jimmy's head as he stood on his hind legs and sniffed at the counter. The little dog's patient brown eyes were not unlike Amanda's own.

"Well," said William, blankly, "I am; yes, I—I"—

"On business, I presume; what is your line?" said Amanda, wishing to be agreeable. "Are you in the dentistry business?"

"Well, no," said the new postmaster, frowning very much with bewilderment; "no, I can't say I am. Not dentistry, exactly; no. I came down to call, ma'am, on you. You are Mrs. Gedge, I presume. I understand you run this office."

Amanda Gedge felt a sudden contraction about her heart. "The post-office belongs to mother," she said, faintly. The numb and hidden terror of the past weeks confronted her and clamored for a hearing.

"Yes, just so; so I understood," said William Sprague. "Well, perhaps you weren't looking for me before the 1st, but I thought I'd come; I thought I 'd get to know the place, ma'am."

William took off his hat and wiped his forehead. He wished he had a bit of stick and his knife, then he would not have to look at her, he thought; the slow whitening of her face; the movement of her dry lips as she tried to speak and could not; her hands clutching the edge of the counter until the knuckles were white, and her changed voice, were terrible. It was like seeing some poor, dumb creature tortured.

"What — what? I don't know — I don't know — what you mean?"

"Well, I 've been put in here, you know," William said, bending down to pull Jimmy's ears, so that he need not see her face; "and I came along now to Pennyville because I thought, perhaps, you 'd — I 've no experience, and I thought " — He began to stammer with pity; her rigid face and wide, terror-stricken brown eyes confused him. "I hope you are well, and your ma, too," he ended, weakly.

"You will kill mother," said Amanda.

"Ma'am?"

"You will kill her if you turn her out of her post-office."

William Sprague shuffled his feet noisily on the floor; then he took off his hat and seemed to scan it critically. "I ain't responsible, Miss

Gedge; I was sent here. The department decided to make a change, I suppose, and I was
sent here."

"You must go away," Amanda said; her
voice broke, and she could not say anything
more.

William's eyes glistened. "This is the cus-
sedest business I was ever in," he said, under
his breath. "Poor girl! Poor thing!" He
felt something roll down his cheek, and that
helped him to be angry. "Well," he said,
sternly; "this ain't your affair, nor mine.
I'm sent. I can't help it. I'm to be in on
the first day of May. I'll go away *till* then.
I'd just as lief as not clear out till the first of
the month, if it will oblige you any; honest, I
would."

"Don't you understand?" Amanda explained,
her voice monotonous with pain. "I don't
want you to come back — ever. Mother's
been here twenty years. If she was put out,
she would die. She would be on the town; but
the worst thing to her, the thing that would kill
mother, would be to be put out. Oh, go away!
You can come back when she dies — yes, you
can come back then. Oh, go — *go!*" Amanda
stopped; she dropped her head upon the counter and sobbed aloud.

William wiped his brow and sighed.

Amanda lifted her large face, working with tears. "Mother's been here twenty years," she repeated, — "twenty years."

William Sprague stamped across the post-office and back. "Well, ma'am, I'm sorry. I don't mind saying I'm sorry. I — I — I'm damned sorry! But I don't see what I can do about it. If I wasn't here, somebody else would be. And — well, I'm put here, and it's my duty to stay where I'm put."

"Mother's done her duty," said Amanda, feebly.

"I ain't a-questionin' that, of course," William assured her quickly. "She's all right, of course. But the party has changed, you know. The Democrats are in. Now you and your mother ain't Democrats, so — out you go!"

"What!" cried Amanda, looking at him with sudden hope, "not Democrats? Why, if that's the reason, we'll *be* Democrats! I'll write and tell the President so. Why, we'd just as lief be Democrats, sir. Won't you tell the President so?"

"My Lord!" said William Sprague.

"I'll write to the President. Oh, if that's all, it will be all right. If they had only told us that, we'd have changed in November."

"Well, ma'am," interposed William, wearily, "I guess I'll go up to the hotel and rest a bit, and may be we can talk it over later in the evening. I'll come in and set awhile, and we'll talk it over, and you'll see." William was actually fatigued with the hopelessness of the situation.

"No; mother would wonder," Amanda answered. "I — I will be out, walking down by the bridge, and if you'll be there, I'll explain; I'll tell you why we can't leave, and you'll understand."

VI.

That meeting at the bridge was productive of nothing but the need of another talk, and after it William reflected that he must not leave Pennyville until Amanda was reconciled to his return on the 1st of May, so he settled down comfortably at the tavern. Of course by this time Mrs. Gedge was the only person in the village who did not understand the situation; but everybody united to conceal it from her.

Mr. Sprague was so sympathetic in spite of his quiet determination to "have the place" that he was not greatly disliked, as might have been supposed. He was the unwilling tool of circumstances; he could not — that was very

clear — he could not help himself; "for," as
he explained a dozen times a day, — "for, if
I didn't come, somebody else would, and it
would be just as bad on 'Mandy." William
had adopted the customs of the village at once,
and called everybody by their first names.

A week of protest and insistence slipped by;
to Amanda it was only a long daze of terror;
to the new postmaster it was pitiful but interesting. He was as kind as possible to Amanda; he bought a very hideous little blue glass
dish, in the shape of a shell, and presented it
to her; he even fetched her a bunch of wild
flowers, — London-pride and dog-tooth violets
and Quaker-ladies. Amanda took them list-
lessly. She explained to her mother that the
gentleman who was stopping up at the tavern
— "that big red man you saw on the stage, who
comes to the office 'most every day with his
dog" — he had given her the presents, she said.

Mrs. Gedge revived with this new interest,
like some poor, faded flower that looks up for a
moment in the rain. "Why, child," she said,
her black eyes fairly snapping with pleasure,
"you've got a beau! I think you might ask
him into the parlor some time, 'Mandy, to see
me."

William Sprague made this same suggestion.
"I'd like to see your ma, 'Mandy; course I

won't say a word to her, but I 'd just like to see how the land lays."

And so Amanda had no choice but to arrange a meeting. "Will you come in this afternoon?" she said; and Mr. Sprague assented at once.

Mrs. Gedge, when she heard that he was coming, was filled with excited hospitality, and made her daughter wheel her immediately into the parlor. "He 'll be here in two or three hours, child," she said, "so you just get to work and dust up. Open the shutters first. Now, come, be spry! Dear! if I had my legs!" Almost with irritation she watched Amanda, moving slowly about with the duster in heavy silence. Amanda was not excited. "It 's like a girl," Mrs. Gedge thought. "They take their beaux for granted, and won't make a speck of effort for 'em! But 'Mandy ain't as young as she was; she ought to take pains." When the shutters were opened, she felt a pang as she saw a strip of sunshine stretching across the red and blue roses of the carpet. "It will fade it," she thought; "but there! if 'Mandy takes him, I guess he can buy her a new carpet one of these days."

The dreary order of the room was really perfect; there was nothing to be done except to wait impatiently for the arrival of the caller.

An hour before he was expected, Mrs. Gedge put on her best cap; it was almost new, for she had not worn it a half-dozen times since Amanda made it four years ago; then she shook out the folds of a clean handkerchief, and drew Amanda's blue plaid shawl about her shoulders. Then a happy thought struck her. " 'Mandy, I believe that those black mitts of mine are in that old cigar-box, in the right-hand corner, back, of my top bureau drawer. Do look, 'Mandy. There, child, hurry! My, you ain't fast, are you?"

Amanda found the little black silk mitts, and then wheeled her mother's chair upon the braided mat before the empty fireplace, just as William Sprague lifted the knocker on the front door. It was so long since that door had been opened that the key would not turn in the lock, and Amanda, in an embarrassed voice, was obliged to call out to Mr. Sprague, "Will you please go round to the kitchen door, and come in that way?" This was mortifying; but the occasion was too great and too agreeable for mortifications to be long remembered; and Mr. Sprague certainly did not seem put out by it, Mrs. Gedge said afterwards.

He found the little crippled old woman sitting up very straight in her chair, with her mitts crossed carefully in front of her, and the ruffle of her cap fairly quivering with pleasure. The sunshine had crept round to the west window, so that the lilac bushes kept most of it from the carpet, and, free from that anxiety, Mrs. Gedge could give herself up to the opportunity of the moment.

"Praise to the face is open disgrace," she said, smiling and nodding, in answer to Mr. Sprague's remark that Miss 'Mandy seemed real smart, housekeeping and running a post-office, too, — "Praise to the face is open disgrace, but I must say the child *is* capable. She's a real smart girl, sir."

Amanda stood with a stony face behind her mother's chair. As William said "post-office" she looked up, and her tired eyes besought him with a quick terror; he nodded, reassuringly.

"I should think, now, Mrs. Gedge," he began, "you and Miss 'Mandy would be about tired of the office, you've been there so long; honest, I would."

Mrs. Gedge was hospitable and condescending, but she could not allow any such talk as that; she smiled primly, and her voice was less friendly. "No, sir," she said; "in our position we cannot think of ourselves. We are glad, 'Mandy and me, to be in the service, and I'm sure we couldn't be so unworthy as to think of being tired. Besides that," she ended, trying to be less severe, "'Mandy really takes a good deal off me. 'Mandy's real capable."

"But you've been here a good while," William insisted, anxiously; he was not making his point as he had hoped to; he looked about the room in a shifting, embarrassed way; he wished he had not come.

"Yes; 'Mandy was only twenty-five," returned Mrs. Gedge, cheerfully; "'t was a good bit ago, but 'Mandy has kept her looks. There, child, you need n't poke my shoulder. I guess your mother can say that. You've been a real good girl, 'Mandy, too. Well, now, sir, how do you like Pennyville?"

William found this much more comfortable ground, even though Mrs. Gedge, in the most delicate way in the world, said that she understood he was a widower, and of course it was lonely for him in a strange place like Pennyville, and she hoped he'd come often to see her and 'Mandy.

"You'll always be real welcome, sir," she assured him. "In our position we have n't much time, we are so occupied; but I'm sure we'll be glad to do anything we can for you," she ended, with friendly patronage. "Won't we, 'Mandy?"

"Yes, mother," said Amanda, faintly.

Mrs. Gedge made a little impatient cluck be-

tween her teeth; it was real silly for Amanda
to be so shy, she thought. She enjoyed this
visit very much, but she was tired when at
last her guest said good-by. As for William
Sprague, he went away with a very sober face.

It was only a few days now until the change
must be made. Amanda had altered so that
Mrs. Gedge would have been alarmed but for
this delightful interest of the beau. Not that
she named Mr. Sprague thus to Amanda; she
asked every conceivable question about him,
but she nursed her little hope in silence, with
small chuckles when she was alone, and with
knowing looks and nods when the neighbors
came in to gossip. She was too interested and
pleased with this very personal happiness to
notice any constraint in the talk of Sally Goodrich, or Mrs. Dace, or any one else; but there
was constraint. All the village joined Amanda
in shielding Mrs. Gedge as long as possible
from the dreadful knowledge that threatened
her.

The 1st of May was on Monday. On Thurs-
day Amanda, her face set in haggard silence,
went up to the graveyard. She had decided to
tell her mother the next morning. There was
nothing to hope for now; her frantic appeal
to the department had only been answered by
a brief assurance of her mother's inefficiency.

Once, before that assurance came, she lay awake all night to plan a visit to Washington. She could take some of Mrs. Gedge's one hundred dollars out of the bank and go. She would make some excuse to her mother, so that she might not guess the humiliating truth. Yes, she would see the President; she would tell him. But the very next day came that brief, decided answer from Washington that left her nothing to hope for from the Government.

William Sprague, stolidly, but with the kindest pity in his twinkling, anxious eyes, assured her that there was nothing to hope for from any other quarter. She felt no resentment towards William; she believed him implicitly when he told her it was not his fault. No, he could not help it; he had been sent.

She would go and sit by Willie awhile, she said to herself, as she toiled wearily up the hill, and plan what she should do when the check from Washington ceased to come. There was a hundred dollars in the bank at Mercer, from which Mrs. Gedge received four dollars and fifty cents a year; that was all. They owned their house, but it was of no value save as a shelter. No one would buy or rent it. Everybody had a house of his own, — everybody except Mr. Sprague, and he had at once announced his determination to live in the tavern.

that being cheaper and more comfortable than housekeeping for a single man. Amanda could sew, but who would give her work? All the women in Pennyville did their own sewing, and Mrs. Dace helped them with the rare occurrence of a new dress. She could go up to the tavern and help Mrs. Thyme in the summer; but at two dollars a week for twelve weeks — at the very most, Mr. Thyme's summer boarders did not stay longer than twelve weeks — she could only earn twenty-four dollars.

Amanda thought this all out, sitting there by Willie, her elbows on her knees, her chin in her hands, and her eyes staring blankly at a dead mullein-stalk swaying in the wind. If she went away to work, went to town, she might keep her mother from the almshouse; yes, that was what she must do. She must take her to Mercer; take her away from friends and neighbors; away from the old home. "Oh, I wish mother might die before she knew it," this old daughter said from her aching heart. Yes, by taking her to town, she might keep her from the poorhouse; but oh, there was no way to save the heart-break, the pride that must be trampled down, the violence of leaving the home to which Adam Gedge had brought his bride, and in which Amanda had been born and little Charles had died, — the misery of transplanted age! Amanda had no more tears, but she drew in her breath in a sort of moan. She found herself wondering at those days of anxiety about the album. How could she have been worried over so little a thing? Ah, how gladly would she exchange this new despair for the old pain! Amanda sat upright and wrung her hands.

"'Mandy!" some one shouted from the road. It was William Sprague; he was slipping the leather loop from over the gate-post, and pushing the old, sagging gate back across the grass. "I want to speak to you, 'Mandy," he said, in his loud, cheerful voice. "Your mother said she believed you was up here. If you don't mind, I'll talk to you a bit." He had reached her by this time, and stood watching her with friendly concern. Jimmy came and sniffed her hand, and then licked it with his little rough tongue. Amanda did not notice him, and William shook his head. "Why," he thought, much impressed, "she don't see Jimmy! 'Mandy," he said, "I've thought of something. It isn't perhaps just the thing you'd like, but it's the only thing I can think of. And I'm willing. Well, I — I'd really like it, 'Mandy."

Amanda looked at him, her lips parted, and with dilated eyes.

"If we was to get married?" said William, and paused.

Amanda Gedge did not seem to understand him; she made no answer.

"You see, it's like this: Your ma 'd be pleased, and she'd never know anything. I'd have a home, and I'd be comfortable. And I don't mind being married at all; honest, I'd just as lief. And I like you, 'Mandy. It's only fair to say that. I told your ma I liked you, and I was coming up here to tell you so. So let 's get married."

"You told mother?" said Amanda, in a whisper. Her heart beat so that it seemed as though she could not breathe.

"You have n't thought that way about me, I know," he said, apologetically; "but look at it, 'Mandy; it will make it all right for the old lady, and we can't make it all right any other way. We 've got to arrange it between our-selves, — me and you and your mother. And, honest, I can't see any other way out of it; and I think you 're a real nice girl, 'Mandy. I like you — so I do. Now, if you can only just make up your mind to me?"

Amanda Gedge put her hand down on the grass as though she were groping for some other hand to help her. "Oh, what shall I do?" she said.

William Sprague sat down beside her, and then remembered the imprudence of sitting on the grass in April, and rose. "I thought it all out," he assured her, "and it come to me last night all of a sudden. ' Well, there! ' says I to myself, ' and we neither of us thought of it! ' But it 's the only thing to do. It will straighten out everything. What do you say, 'Mandy?"

But she had nothing to say. She saw the bit of dim glass in the slate headstone, and caught the last line of the inscription, "Mourned by his friends." She put her hands over her face. "Oh, *Willie!*" she said.

"Well, now, there! that 's right," said William, heartily. "My first wife called me that, and I like to hear it again. We 'll get along first rate, 'Mandy, — me and you and Jimmy and the old lady. Come, now, it 's all settled, ain't it?"

She drew a half-sobbing breath before she could speak. " I don't know — I don't know! I think I 'll go home now, Mr. Sprague. I thank you; indeed I do; but I must see mother. I must go home. Oh, it will save mother. Oh, you are very kind to think of it — William."